DOTY MEETS
COYOTE

For Elizabeth

Thom Doty

DOTY MEETS
COYOTE
THOMAS DOTY

BLACKSTONE
PUBLISHING

Copyright © 2016 by Thomas Doty
Produced by Jason R. Couch
Published in 2016 by Blackstone Publishing
Cover photograph by Melani Marx
Cover design by Alenka Linaschke
Series design by Kathryn Galloway English
Illustrations by Thomas Doty

Printed in the United States of America

First Printing, 2016

ISBN 978-1-5047-0832-6

1 2 3 4 5 6 7 8 9 10

Blackstone Publishing
31 Mistletoe Rd.
Ashland, OR 97520

www.Downpour.com

TABLE OF CONTENTS

ANCESTORS AND ELDERS

MY NAME IS THOMAS DOTY. I AM a Native American storyteller. My family background is Takelma, Shasta, Irish, and English. My connection to my native roots was strengthened over the years by listening to stories my grandmother told me, from gazing at old family photos and taking family trips to native sites. And time spent with Native American elders, including Chuck Jackson, who taught me much about our native traditions, and Caraway George, who first took me to my ancestral village of Coyote's Paw. He told me, "We have a tribal memory of your ancestors living here." Except for some time at Reed College in Portland and some extended jaunts to England, Ireland, and Alaska, I have lived in southern Oregon all of my life, where my ancestors have lived for generations.

Winter is the season of native storytelling. On long nights, during the moon called Shoulder to Shoulder Around the Fire, people gather in community houses and share stories. Old Time stories are remembered, new ones created, each story deepening the homeland roots of the people. Gaukos becomes the moon. Coyote steals fire. A father tries to bring his dead daughter back from the Land of the Dead. As storms scream through the village, people sit close to the fire sharing stories, night after winter night.

Each time I tell stories, I thank those storytellers who kept the stories alive for centuries.

It is my work as a storyteller to not only perpetuate the Old Time myths with integrity, but to add new stories to the collective basket of folklore, just as tellers before me have done for a long, long time. Storytelling is an ancient tradition as well as a living art.

As I started sharing native stories in the 1980s, I listened to elders and learned from them: Chuck Jackson, Caraway George, Edison Chiloquin. I poured through reams of field notes from linguists and anthropologists who collected stories from elders who would soon become ancestors: Frances Johnson, Molly Orton, Sargent Sambo. And over the years I became friends with elders I continue to learn from: Agnes Baker-Pilgrim, John Medicine Horse Kelly, and so many others.

Here in the West, much of our native mythology was fractured in the 1800s. With the arrival of Europeans, disease, war, and following the many Trails of Tears to the reservations, many of our stories and cultural traditions were scattered to the winds.

When I was a young college student, I immersed myself in the writing of the Irish poet W. B. Yeats. It impressed me that through his poems, plays, essays and collections of folk and fairy tales, he helped bring Irish mythology back to the Irish people. His work became a model for my own life's work: putting our traditional myths back together as well as creating new stories that dramatize our culture, our history, our folklore . . . bringing our local mythology back to the people. And making the stories available to everyone: to those who celebrate their Native American heritage, to those who feel native through their deep connection to culture and place, to those who are experiencing the wisdoms of native stories for the first time.

Thank you, ancestors and elders, for the stories you have passed along. I feel honored to continue your work.

GRANDMA MAUDE

For me, storytelling began with my grandmother. Grandma Maude was our family storyteller. She gathered us children around the pot-bellied stove and told us stories . . . stories from our native ancestors who are Takelma and Shasta from where I live in southern Oregon, stories from our Irish and English ancestors who settled in the Rogue Valley in the 1800s, and stories from this amazing landscape we have called home for a long, long time.

Grandma Maude was a large woman. She didn't move around much. But she had a wonderfully rich voice and different voices for animals in the stories. And her hands were so expressive that they invited stories into the room. Those stories became our good friends.

Though Grandma journeyed into the next world when I was young—I was only nine years old—I have never forgotten her stories. And I hear her voices, all of them, inside my own stories.

Grandmother

In honor of grandmothers, I share these words.

you grandmother
you creek
foaming away and away
down the hills to the sea

I want to slant a tree
across your flowing
slow you down
make a pond

dive deep and deeper
under the froth
till the spring flooding

the current
all yellow with pollen
shakes loose
the log dam

takes you and me
away and away
where the sea and the sky
foam together

SUN AND STORIES COME INTO THE WORLD TOGETHER

On the darkest nights of the year, the people tell this story.

A long time ago there was a time when the people living here along the river had no sunlight. There was no sun at all. The people lived in this cold, dark village, so cold it was hard to keep warm, so dark it was hard to find food. They couldn't see anything. They couldn't see the mountains and lakes, the rivers and forests. Though they walked a long ways downriver, they couldn't see the ocean. And because they couldn't see these places, the people had no stories about them. But the people were smart. The people have always been smart. They knew these places were out there. They smelled the salt from the ocean. They listened to the wind in the trees in the forests. They heard the rushing of creeks down the mountains. But the people had no stories, and the people had no sunlight.

One day the people gathered in their cold, dark place and somebody said, "We should have sunlight." Somebody else said, "Hmmmmm, good idea." Some grumpy fellow said, "It's all very good to talk, but who is going to be the sun?"

Nobody volunteered right away. It's not an easy job to be the sun. No one, that is, except Raven. Mister Raven, that great, black bird. Raven, who thinks so much of himself. When Raven heard the people ask for the sun, he pointed at his own silly face and he answered, "Raven will be the sun, of course! Haaaaa! Raaaaaven!"

He imagined himself looking beyond grand, rising and setting, rising and setting, his black wings covering the people. He would own the light. No one would see anything on the earth or in the sky without the presence of sun-master Raven.

He rose out of the deep night. He shook his shabby wings, flapping them again and again. But no light came. Days were shadowed with evening. The woods were deep and dark. The river was a black pool without a bottom. The people groaned, "Get out of the sky, you witless bird. You are too black!"

The people gathered again in their cold, dark village and said to each other, "Someone else must be the sun."

Hawk screeched in his shrill voice, "I shall be the sun!"

He imagined rising up higher than anyone had ever gone. He would make the people so small they would no longer be people. He would be himself in the roof of the sky, higher than the wind could climb. He would be so huge and bright that his shadow would be the only shadow. No one else would matter.

As he rose out of the night, he filled the sky. The air turned bright as he soared, brilliant as he climbed to the height of midday. His wings were too bright to look at. He screamed as he flashed and spread his talons and reached for more light. The people squinted and screamed, "You are too bright! We cannot see a thing! Go somewhere else, you selfish Hawk!"

The people were getting depressed. They were tired and cold. They gathered again and said, "Someone must be the sun."

There was Coyote. Mister Coyote, who also thinks a great deal of himself. When Coyote heard the people ask for someone to be the sun, he howled back at himself, "Coyoteee! Heheheheheeeee! Coyoooooteeeee!"

He imagined dancing his dog dance as he pounced over the people, tricking them, scaring them, sending them diving onto the frozen earth. There would be no escape from the tricks of this master trickster. In an instant he shifted his thoughts from ice to fire and howled in delight at his new plan.

He rose out of the depths of darkness. He ran fast as a flash across the village, too fast to see, so fast he left a trail of heat behind him. He leaped higher and his trail turned hotter. He spit fire, and the night turned into a blazing day that singed and scorched.

The people slipped in their own sweat. Their lungs were raw with heat and smoke. They dove into the river!

"You are cooking everything! Get out of the sky, you hot-headed Coyote!!"

The people gathered one last time in their cold, dark village, shivering on the edge of hopelessness. They muttered, "We're done for. No sun will come to our village."

But Snake whispered, "I had a dream that I was the sun."

Raven and Hawk and Coyote made fun of him. They said, "You cannot run or jump. You cannot screech or bark. You cannot scorch, brighten, or even thaw the frozen earth. How can a spineless Snake be the sun?"

Snake spoke softly. "By knowing I can, by dreaming I can."

As he rose out of the night, he grabbed his tail in his mouth and made a circle. And slowly, very slowly, he shed his skin and gently made the dawn, all red and orange. He shed his skin again and midday was full of blue sky. Another skin made a beautiful sunset with more colors than the people had ever imagined. And at night, when darkness returned, Snake shed one more skin. He watched from a distance as the people slept in their houses. The people dreamed of Snake rising again in the dawn, and when Snake returned, a new day began.

That was the day sunlight came to the people.

The people could see! They saw the mountains and lakes, the river and forests. They saw the ocean. The people made wonderful stories about these places, places that would be very important to them for thousands of years.

That was the beginning of stories. The Old Ones passed this story to us, and that's how we've been telling it for a long, long time.

DOTY MEETS COYOTE

There I go, wandering from town to town, weaving tales of Coyote and Bear and Bluejay. It has always been my dream—the dream of any storyteller worth his salted salmon—to "become" the stories I tell.

Someday I'll disappear into the wilderness, the heart of where stories come from. Folks in town will tell stories of a long-haired, wild-eyed fellow as completely at home in the woods as Raven or Skunk, this mad spirit of stories who waylays weary hikers and tells them myths so vivid, so alive, that animal and human shapes leap out of their campfires and dance in their minds. My stories will be so much a part of the woods that at the end I'll disappear into the shadows of trees without a trace, my words drifting through the wood smoke. This is my dream to be a story.

So imagine my joy when one day near my hometown of Ashland, where the town ends and the woods begin, I get a long look at a coyote as he crosses my path and saunters into the woods. Not just any scraggly and curious coyote, but the scraggly and curious Coyote of story fame, that doggy buffoon and chief trickster, that out-of-focus mirror of humankind.

I pause and ponder the possibilities. Is this pooch my guide to realizing my dream? I shake my head and free myself of the moment. I start to walk home.

But this isn't the end. Coyote is always up to something. He follows me, lurking in the trees, listening, watching, until he can't stand it anymore. He leaps onto my path and howls, "Hold up! Hold up! You just get to the best part and quit? Maybe you need a little rest in the country. Sit down and be quiet and I'll finish this story.

"So Doty takes a step beyond his dream of becoming a story. He meets the lifeblood of myth, the dramatist of truth, the most handsome, intelligent fellow ever put into words, the unkillable, enduring bringer of good fortune, this well-groomed charmer of wit, this life of the eternal party of wisdom—me!—Mister Coyote myself.

"So Coyote, taking pity on Doty, lowers his standards and allows the lesser wordsmith to accompany him on his travels, adventure after adventure. They head out of town, Doty stupidly but happily trotting behind."

So begins the friendship of me and Coyote, the storyteller and the story, a friendship as old as the woods.

I'm still working on becoming my stories. One thing I know: with legendary Coyote along for the ride, my dream has become a journey through the landscape of Mythtime, where anything is possible. So far, it's been a wild and wonderful journey.

That evening, Coyote and I drive in my rig from our Rogue Valley home along the curves of a mountain road and into the cradle of the Cascade Mountains.

In my home, there is a photograph of me sitting on a log in a forest next to a blazing fire. It is twilight. There is a silhouette of firs and pines behind me, and through the trees is the purple shimmer of Lake of the Woods, and beyond that the wild wilderness of the Cascades. I am long-haired and long-bearded. I am wearing a muslin shirt and jeans faded in the knees, and I am barefoot. It is July, and I am just a few months old as a storyteller.

The fire flares and sends sparks dancing whirligigs. My eyes shine wild. A few feet beyond the circle of firelight, nearly invisible in the shadows of the forest, is Coyote. He whispers to me, "Are you sure you want to do this? In a few minutes an entire Scout troop of adolescent boys will clamor into this picture and plop themselves down and expect to be, at the least, entertained with stories. One will make some sort of noise that only boys think is funny and the rest will snicker. I hear they can be a tough audience."

"No problem," I say. "I'll just give them what they want."

"What's that?"

"Something about girls, of course. And you're in it!"

"All right!" howls Coyote. "I'm all ears. Quiet now, I think I hear them coming."

In a cloud of trail dust and flashlights and shouting, thirty boys roar into the firelight. They mostly settle into silence—save a few snickers—and the photograph comes alive as I start my story.

A long, long time ago Coyote was living near Klamath Lake, where he could see Llao Yaina, the mountain that was there before Crater Lake was made. He was living in an open meadow near the lake so he could watch the night sky.

Coyote loved watching the stars. All night long he'd stick his snout into the air and watch the stars walk across the sky, their trails making big arcs. Now Coyote always saw what he wanted to see. So he watched all those stars sticking out their chests and their noses, making a fine walking sound: badoop ... badoop ... badoop ...

One night Coyote noticed a large star, a good looking star. She was more beautiful than the sun, even more beautiful than the moon. And the star was flashy. She flashed colors: yellows and reds. She was a good looking star.

Coyote likes flashy women. He's that kind of dog. So he kept watching her, night after night after night, all night long, thinking, "Wowee! That's a knockout of a star!"

Five nights went by and he started talking to her. But she never answered him. Not one word. She walked across the sky: badoop ... badoop ...

badoop … She looked way down on little Coyote—he was just a ball of fur down on the earth—but she wouldn't utter a peep.

Coyote started getting wild around the eyes, his eyes bugging out a long ways. He started going crazy for that star. He walked around with his tongue wagging, his eyes bulging, saying, "Look at that star! Is she not a good looking star? Look how she walks, all flashy and everything. And look where she goes, so close to the top of that big mountain. Why, I could run up there, reach up and grab her."

Coyote thought that was a great idea. He started running. He ran and he ran all through the night, his tongue wagging the whole way. He ran all the next day, his tongue starting to droop a bit, and by late afternoon, he was all the way up the mountain, his tongue dragging the dirt. He was beyond tired.

But he was thinking of that star. "Well, I better not go to sleep. I might miss her. I've missed some pretty good things by sleeping too much. I'll just walk back and forth on top of this mountain. That will keep me awake."

So he paced back and forth across the mountain, covering the peak with his tracks. A long while went by, or so it seemed to Coyote.

"This is taking forever. A person as important as I am shouldn't have to wait so long. Besides, I really hate waiting for women. Makes my paws all sweaty."

Coyote kept pacing. Pacing and waiting. Pacing and waiting. Then suddenly he stopped.

He bugged his eyes. "Look there. The sun's going down. And there come the stars. One there, another over there. And look, those stars aren't walking across the sky making that silly badoop noise. Those stars are dancing tonight, right across the sky!"

Coyote went to the edge of the peak to get a better look.

"Wowee! There she is. My star. She's even better looking up close. And she's dancing my way."

Coyote went to the highest place on the peak. "I'd better make myself a little better looking. This is a big-time date." He started smoothing down his fur, straightening his tail, picking old food out of his teeth, rinsing his armpits with his tongue. "Nothing worse than Coyote pits on a first date." He worked and he worked, getting himself all spruced up and slicked down.

Now the star danced toward Coyote.

"Come on, star," whispered Coyote. "Dance a little closer. That's it. Closer and closer."

When the star was as close to Coyote as she was going to get, Coyote leaped into the air, panting, his tongue wagging, arms stretching up and up and up … but he couldn't reach her.

"Hey, star! Reach down your hands. Take me up there with you. I can't quite reach you. This is powerful lover-boy Coyote talking. Reach down and take me up there with you."

The star reached down, grabbed Coyote by his sweaty paws, and they started dancing together up from the mountain.

They danced higher and higher into the sky, way over the earth.

Up high, it was bitter cold. And quiet. None of those stars ever said a word.

Poor Coyote had never been up that high before. He was feeling dizzy, his eyeballs dancing around, and he was holding onto his stomach, trying to keep his last meal from flying out all over the place.

The star went higher and higher.

Coyote called out, "Hey, some of you other stars, this is powerful Coyote talking. Take me back down to the earth. I don't do so well up here. I think I'm going to get sick all over the sky. Take me back down!"

The star held on tight.

They danced higher and higher and higher. When they got to that cold place at the top of the sky, the star let go of Coyote.

She dumped him. Dumped him out of the sky. Dumped him out of love.

Now Coyote was falling like a furry comet, his eyes bugging out and flashing, his tail flying behind. People on the ground were watching. "Hey, look at that stupid Coyote falling out of the sky. Just the sort of thing he'd do just to get attention."

Coyote fell and fell, picking up speed, getting closer to the earth. He was coming down on top of that mountain Llao Yaina.

And SPLAT!

At the bottom of the mountain was Mister Bear. The splat of Coyote's liquid impact woke him up. Curious, though a little sleepy and more than a little grumpy, he climbed to what was left of the peak to have a look at things.

"That's Coyote all right," mumbled Bear in his slow, contemplative way. "He's hit the top of the mountain and made a big hole. And all that Coyote blood squirted and squished around until this hole was filled up with blood and bones and ears and eyeballs and fur and all of Coyote's parts. Looks like Coyote stew."

Mister Bear started ambling back down the mountain, still muttering to himself, "But not the kind you'd want to eat. Or smell. Or even get close to. Yuk!" Bear got disgusted and ambled faster.

Rain came, and cold weather, freezing rain and snow. Years and years of rain and snow filled the hole and slowly turned that big bowl of Coyote stew into water. It made a beautiful, deep-blue lake.

People nowadays call that lake Crater Lake, up in the Klamath country.

If you go to Crater Lake late at night, you might see Coyote's sons and daughters and grandchildren, all sitting on the rim above the lake, their snouts pointing to the sky, their mouths yapping away.

They're scolding the star that killed their grandfather that long time ago.

I once heard a storyteller add a little epilogue to this story, and I share it with the boys.

"Hey, Coyote! There's that flashy star again. She's a luscious babe, and tonight she's dancing close to that mountain, her tasty colors and lickable curves just out of reach. A delicious masquerade, a sweet-talking lure without the words. You've got that peckish, toe-tapping look in your eyes. You've puffed up the slope to the peak. You're ready to make the leap and whirl into the light fantastic. By now your gut is growling and you've forgotten how you suffer the messy results for the sake of your dance. You know what everyone says? Coyote is a reassembly-required kind of dog! And to boot, you're the untiring clichés you can never remember. What are they? Dance like no one is watching? Love like you've never been hurt? Hunger works just as well, right, old friend? Good luck, Mister Coyote! Gorge yourself on the moment! See you in the next story when you've put yourself back together. There you go! Yummy!!"

I tell stories through most of the night. One by one, sleepy boys sneak across camp and crawl into their sleeping bags, heading toward vivid dreams that come only after one has spent time in the forests, along the pebbly shores of these mountain lakes, high in the Cascades, and after nights of listening to stories by firelight. As they slip toward sleep, the boys whisper to each other about the animal shapes the flames and shadows seemed to make move and how brilliant the stars are. But within each cluster of sleeping bags the conversation eventually finds its way to the topic of girls, and there is no lack of snickering and giggling until the woods once again become silent, save the few sounds made by night critters who call this place home. Coyote and I—the pooch quite pleased to have heard an entire evening of stories about himself—crawl into our sleeping bags next to the fire. Soon I am snoozing and Coyote snoring, and in these few hours before the early rising of the summer sun, the mountain stars dance their circle dance, the shadows of the woods whisper their wisdoms, and there are more dreams in this forest than even the trees can remember.

When I was a boy, I helped build a footbridge across Dry Creek at that same camp at Lake of the Woods.

The bridge was at the junction of several trails. One led to the marsh where I watched pelicans dip for trout, another to the summit of Mount McLoughlin. Down yet another trail I made the memorable mistake of killing a frog. The camp rule was: you kill it, you eat it. And I did.

Thirty years later, my memory connects the trails. I smell the dust of summer hiking, hear the chatter of trail talk. A breeze ripples the surface, blurring the lily-pad bottom.

Thirty years later, this bridge spans more than water.

Coyote and I traipse across the footbridge and head up the long trail that winds and winds through thick forests, curves around mountain lakes, and finally zigzags in switchbacks to the summit of Mount McLoughlin.

The Takelma name for this mountain is Wilamxa, "The Floating Mountain."

Upon a time it floated through clouds of creation. Then, under a boiling fume of ash and steam, it settled onto the Cascades and became the home of white-haired Acorn Woman. Every snowmelt she hangs her swelling skin on the oak trees and grows acorns, and every winter she sleeps on her mountain. Her white hair is the shape of the snow.

Since I was eleven, I have walked this trail many times. From the summit I have watched the shadow of the mountain float over forests and lakes. And sleeping there, I dreamed I was floating among stars.

At ninety-five-hundred feet, in dreams and shifts of the landscape, the old myths get retold.

After puffing and whining, grumbling and groaning, Coyote and I scramble up the basalt spine of the mountain, up the last thousand yards to the top.

From the heights of clouds, our world is a circle. We see the Rogue Valley that is our home and imagine, not far beyond, the blue Pacific reaching to the west. We see the immense and snowy height of Mount Shasta and the brown and rumpled hills of California's Central Valley to the south, the nearby jagged thrust of Devil's Peak, the basalt rim of Crater Lake, and the white peaks of the Cascades stepping to the north. We look east beyond the mountain lakes to Upper Klamath Lake on the edge of a high desert that stretches from the Medicine Lake Volcano to Newberry Caldera, and east into the dry, blue desert haze of distant horizons.

After several minutes of looking around, a few more of near-silent contemplation broken only by ooohs and ahhhs, my canvas bag catches Coyote's eye and he says, "So what's that bundle of notebooks you've got in your satchel? You never seem to be without them."

"These are my scribblings, my collected works, everything from scratches of ideas to poems and stories—storyteller stuff. To us storytellers, our notebooks are the raw material for stories, and, of course, that modern version of salted salmon: paychecks."

"It seems quite a lot of work to haul that stuff up here to the top of the world. Let me give you a piece of advice. We mythic creatures carry stories around in our heads. If you could learn to do that, you would find the burden weighs far less and you'll avoid back problems in your old age."

"I'll work on it," I say.

"But since you did go to all that trouble," says Coyote, "it seems only natural that you might share something from one of your notebooks. We Coyotes like words and stories and all that stuff, and, well, here we are sitting right on top of a story herself, Ms. Acorn Woman. You got anything about her?"

"All right, friend, I will read you a piece I wrote on this very spot a number of years ago. Ready?"

"Ready."

From the summit of Mount McLoughlin, I scatter a friend's ashes to the wind. Ash drifts over the Cascade landscape of forests and lakes, some settling onto the peak and mixing with volcanic ash, which looks strikingly the same.

A Shasta storyteller once said, "Some people in the stories turned into mountains. When people dig tunnels, they find their bones."

In a Takelma myth, the Table Rocks were once dragonfly brothers. Sexton Mountain was a dancer. Acorn Woman became Mount

McLoughlin. And Koomookumpts, the Modoc creator, sleeps inside the remnants of an underwater volcano.

The ashes of my friend who was once a person drift over the Cascades and into my memory, like a story.

"So who was this friend?" asks Coyote.

"My teacher, of course, the fellow who taught me about stories. Everything I know about storytelling I learned from him, and now he's gone and become part of the mountain. He's become his own story."

The only sounds are the summer wind rushing across the peak and the breathing of two friends sharing the thin air. It would be more within Coyote's character to make some rude, Coyote-like remark, but he holds his tongue. The July sun beams warmth to where we sit. Cascade peaks surround us and define our world, and far, far below, between the floating shadow of the mountain and the more wispy shadows of clouds, lakes and forests shimmer in their summer skins of blue and green.

In the fall, after several months of sauntering around the West telling and collecting and sharing stories, Coyote and me are back in the familiar pine-and-fir smell of the Cascades, and we stop by the camp on our way home. At sunset, Mount McLoughlin flares red—a rich autumn red—as if the molten lava of thousands of years ago still streams down her flanks, burns and smokes its way through the woods, and hisses as it reaches the glowing ripples of the lake.

We stand on the footbridge. New ice reflects clouds swirled into strange shapes by a chilly fall-to-winter wind. Lily pads droop and seem sleepy. The ice is so thin we see the dim shapes of rainbow trout dozing in watery depths made murky by fallen leaves and a long, dusty summer.

I scribble into my notebook …

In November I return to the bridge on Dry Creek at Lake of the

Woods. Remembering my childhood, I visited here last July when the lake was full of ducks and pelicans and geese, the trees full of leaves, and the brimming creek running clear.

Now, fallen leaves stain the creek amber. Waterfowl have arrowed south. And standing on the bridge, I feel a chill to the breeze.

In this stark landscape my mind moves beyond the gathering storm clouds, beyond cold nights freezing the creek to a standstill, beyond snowdrifts that cover the bridge.

My mind moves beyond winter to leaves and ducks and a boy on a bridge, gazing into a clear-running creek.

As snow blows down from the rim of Crater Lake and swirls in clouds around us, Coyote and I walk back to my rig, our coat collars pulled up around our necks. We walk with a silence that shows that we have grown from the ever-streaming conversations of new friends to the more subtle and deep communication of good friends. We start the slow drive down the snow-packed mountain road, through the forests, and back to our cozy home in Ashland.

Crater Lake

*To us native people, Crater Lake is
a beautiful, sacred, powerful place.*

at 8000 feet
lightning strikes close
burns my stomach electric

bolts scorch the lake
crackling and sizzling
flaring the night

2000 feet down
the lake is liquid fire
caldera brimmed with storm
spattering and bubbling
retelling its own myth

early morning stillness
quiet as creation

the world is smooth water
and a breeze cuts a path
for the Maker's canoe

◇◇◇◇◇

we wonder
where the myths come from

a Klamath woman explains

"the black ash fell
and killed the deer
choked the water
smothered our homes

"we knew the mountain
fell in on itself
thousands of years
before the geologists

"we were there
we watched it happen

"then we survived
and made the myths

"creation is primal
like loving
like dying
like birthing

"to keep it alive
we made the stories
and the stories
keep us wondering"

Crater Lake winters are long

from November to June
snowdrifts are deep
blown halfway up
the tallest pines
by winds so fierce
you'd think the mountain
was blowing again

natives come here for power

five winter nights
you get what you came for –
songs from the ice-blue lake
and dialogue with the biting wind

snowmelt in May
starts with a trickle
swelling by June

pine pollen streaks
the blue of the lake
and wildflowers bloom
yellow and red

then the ground dries up
like there wasn't a spring
after the long winter

◇◇◇◇◇

this deep lake
is a good place to love

under stars that flame
like winter fires

breath taut in the thin air
my fingers trace
her lake-smooth skin

loving a native woman
is loving the landscape

ripples of skin moving
mist of her hair across my face
wet kisses of the night

pale morning
stars are coals

breathing long breaths of sleep
we dream in the dew of our sweat
knowing love will go deeper
deep as this lake

◇◇◇◇◇

there are people who remember

in 1984
a Klamath woman said

"we remember the choking ash
we seldom come here
except to seek visions
or to cool off on a hot day"

in 1985
a man with a white cane
stood on the rim of the lake
and said to his wife

"I see nothing
yet everything is here
yes! — a beautiful silence"

then in 1986
an old man danced on the rim
under the mythic moon
under Coyote's star
shifting the night shadows

Crater Lake is primal
there are people who remember

THE WOMAN LOVED TREES

IN THE NATIVE WORLD, EVERYONE IS ALIVE. Everyone is People! There are Animal People, Bird People, Fire People, Human People, and the oldest ones, the Rock People. Many have nicknames. Tree People are affectionately called One Leggeds, Salmon People are Swimmers, Grass People are Dancers. Sometimes, People get lost in translation. Scholars usually translate the village name of Ti'lomikh as "west of which are cedars." From the native point of view it means "west of here live the Cedar People." There are all kinds of People living in the world!

There was a woman who loved trees. When she was a girl she spent days playing in the forest. At night she dreamed she was a Tree Person living deep in the woods. Her neighbors were Cedar and Pine, Fir and Madrone. They knew her well. Together they danced all night to the rhythm of the wind. Their tall shadows shifted and speckled the floor of the forest. All night. Every night. With her friends.

So it made sense to her, when she was grown, that she married one who understood her deeply. One who listened to words the Tree People shared. One who found and set free the stories that lived beneath their bark. This made sense to her. So she married a woodcarver.

They were happy. For a time. While love was a blessing, it was also a distraction. Neither heard the first faint rustlings in the woods. Or sighs in the shadows of their dreams that whispered how short her life would be. When she grew ill, her husband sent for skilled doctors. But no one could help her. On the day she began her journey to the west, the Tree People shed tears to see her go and showered the morning with dew.

Her husband walked in the woods. He wept in the woods. In every tree he saw something that reminded him of his wife. He walked and wept for days.

One morning, he gazed past his tears and ambled into the heart of the forest. He sat down. He listened. He quietly looked around. That tree was tall like his wife. This one had long, dark limbs. That one swayed a certain way in the breeze. He thought he heard her soft voice.

No one tree had all of her features. The woods were a puzzle with the pieces scattered. He wanted to find a way to fit them together. A way to share her story and release his grief. "A carving," he thought. "That's her! That's me!" He stood with purpose, and he walked through the woods toward his home.

THE TRUTHS OF TREES

WHEN I WAS A CHILD, I SPENT many days in my grandparents' home. There was a faded photograph of the redwoods on the wall, above a black rotary-dial telephone. Throughout my childhood I was fascinated with the photo.

One day I tried to make a connection between the telephone and the tall trees. I believed that if I dialed a secret number, I would find myself in the depths of the redwoods or some such magical place. I tried several numbers without success. These attempts ended abruptly when the next phone bill arrived. In my childish way, I suspected that the truth I was seeking was beyond my immediate experience, so I had dismissed local phone numbers early on. Why else would there be so many stories of treks to far-off mystical lands in search of something as worthwhile as truth? I spent a few weeks that summer working off the long distance charges in the family vegetable garden out back.

Out of financial necessity, I searched for new possibilities. The home-made picture frame caught my attention. The photo was framed by many seashells glued together. This was a clue I had overlooked at first, distracted by the telephone's false lure of a direct line to some spirit world. I considered that there must be a connection between the forest and the ocean. Both were vast and limitless, and both left clues in the form of debris: seashells and seaweed on the beach, limbs and shreds of bark on the floor of the forest. There had to be some cosmic reason for the frame to be made of seashells. I squinted and looked past the trees and caught a glimpse of salt spray from a sea wave crashing onto a beach.

In this moment, I knew intuitively that one way into the magic of the trees was through my own imagination. I left the telephone and the picture frame out of my sight and focused on the photo.

In the shadows of redwoods, the leaves of smaller trees and bushes were yellow with fall. Angled shafts of sunlight gave the grove an otherworldly guise. A narrow highway with a faint yellow stripe wandered through the trees, disappearing around a corner beyond where I could see. The road must lead not only through the grove but beyond, to a glimpse of the sea. Beneath the redwoods, the soil looked damp and rich. It came up to the edge of the road and spilled onto it.

This road belonged in these woods. This was a rare instance when I accepted a modern intrusion into an ancient and sacred place. Years later, I protested the building of another road through redwood groves that would have devastated native shrines.

This road of my childhood was a different kind of road. It added the lure of a journey to the photo. Through the length of my youth, I made mental treks into places that invited spiritual contemplation and discovery. This was labeled daydreaming by adults, but I was convinced I knew more than they did. My thoughts were not idle, useless daydreams, but dream-like explorations into the rich beginnings of stories.

I entered the photo and stretched its boundaries beyond the frame. I pursued the fall season into the Mythtime and Dreamtime of winter. I traveled the old highway around the curve through other groves and eventually to the Pacific. My eyes grew wide as I looked up and followed the length of giant trees into coastal fog, where their crowns hid in the damp swirl of a great mystery. I imagined that the tall trees connected this grove to a mirror grove on a planet several galaxies away.

I was convinced that redwoods had a long reach through time and space. They stretched to the stars and back to the beginnings of creation. They had deep roots in their homeland. They were the key to knowing where our oldest stories began. These inner journeys blended with family trips into the redwoods and to the beach. To this day my memories of each are inseparable.

There is truth in trees. As the redwoods are ancient and many, they contain many ancient truths. In Old English the word for tree and truth is the same word: treow. It means to be firm, solid, steadfast. We enter the wilderness looking for truth. We journey into the interior for wisdom. We desire our truths to be steadfast and deeply rooted, and outlast centuries.

Following the deaths of my grandparents, we grandchildren were asked to select things from their home we would like to have as our own. I chose the old photo, and it now hangs in my home next to a window, a fair distance from the telephone. I look at the photo and see the trees of my childhood. I look out the window and see more trees. In each view, I gaze beyond the frame to where the truths of trees reside. One fall day, with yellow leaves still clinging to the oaks near my home, I decide to go searching for the trees in the photo.

Before dawn, I carry a sleepy Coyote out the door of our mountain lair and relocate him to his doggy bed in the backseat of my rig. One eye opens as I lift him and closes when I put him down, and that's the extent of his interest in this journey. "Want to go for a ride?" is a phrase that sends most pooches into tail-wagging, drooling rages of anticipation followed by ear-flapping, wind-barking ecstasy. But not Coyote, unless there's something big in it for himself.

As Coyote dozes on, I head down the road. The Redwood Highway has been widened and paved over again and again, but most redwoods outlast roads, and I am hoping to recognize the giant trees that entranced me as a child. I want to walk into the grove and listen to the stories of the place. In the first faint light of morning, I glance out the car window and the first redwoods come into view.

Coyote wakes up, and his larger-than-life mythic view of himself is stirred. As if drawn to some self-serving satisfaction of conquest that comes from lifting his leg on the largest trees in the world, he whines to be let out. Unlike Steinbeck's French poodle, Charley, who failed to recognize redwoods as trees—they were too big and outside his personal experience—Coyote knows a giant tree when he sees one, and these redwoods are whoppers.

Coyote hits five redwoods in a single round. It doesn't take long to be satisfied with his supremacy, and he is soon curled up in the rig. By the time I stop again, Coyote is asleep. I park on the side of the road near a curve that looks too familiar to pass by. Leaving Coyote snoozing, I walk into the grove as the autumn dawn sends shafts of light angling through the trees.

Light in the redwoods is always dramatic. Creation must have looked like this, dim at first, and damp. Each dawn retells the Tolowa story of the first light streaming through the limbs of the first tree …

There was nothing but water and darkness. The Creator thought the world into existence, and it came floating from the south to its center at Yokokut. The First Redwood grew here, and around its base, the earth was patterned with the tracks of many people: Animal People, Star People, Rock People, Water People, and many more. They were human-like but had characteristics of the beings they would eventually become. They had also been thought into being by the Creator.

When Human People arrived, the others went away and became animals, constellations, rocks, rivers, trees. The Human People settled first at Yokokut, but soon there were many villages in the redwoods, along creeks and rivers and up and down the coast. Each village was the offspring of that first village, and each redwood tree a descendent of the First Redwood.

There was a time when all beings spoke the same language and talked with each other, but now the world has changed and only certain people know how to do this. Sometimes, deep in the groves, those willing to listen hear echoes and whispers of stories and conversations from times long ago.

Each sunrise is the first light after darkness, within each animal is an awareness of the Animal People, each tree is the spirit of the First Redwood, and each dark night filled with rain is a memory from that time before creation when there was nothing but water and darkness. Our ancestors are more than human.

I stand at the edge of the grove. These trees look just like the ones in my photo. No quest is this simple. To us humans, there must be thousands of Tree People who look similar. For the moment, I want to believe that these are the very trees. Leaving the rig and the highway behind, I walk deeper into the grove, and my mind moves into a scene from my childhood …

Midmorning. Clouds roll in from the coast and wrap the trees in mist. The boy Tommy and his cocker spaniel Tippy escape the family hike in the redwoods and go off on their own, deeper into the trees. The hugeness of the redwoods is overwhelming, more than a little boy and his dog can contemplate, but their curiosity draws them deeper in.

They are not just a boy and his pooch. They are mythic heroes in the great playground of their imagination, on a high adventure in the deepest forests of the world. Their village is dying. Everyone is sick. Somewhere deep in the forest is a cure. They were chosen for the quest.

Rain begins. To Tommy and Tippy, this is more than rain. It is a battle of floodwater put in their path by their enemies, those villains who unleashed the deadly sickness on their village.

Tommy and Tippy struggle on against great odds, hungry, exhausted, the rain streaming down and soaking them through. Ahead they see the largest redwood they have ever seen. Its trunk is hollowed out by time, and inside is a room. Using their last bit of energy, they crawl into the heart of the tree's trunk. The dirt floor is covered with the tracks of other critters who have found refuge here. Though it is damp and dark, it is out of the battle of the storm and they feel safe, wrapped in the protection of the tree.

Tommy notices an earthy odor rising from somewhere deep down where the roots live. This is it, he thinks. The medicine to cure the sickness is in the roots of the tree! They have found the elixir, the treasure tree of health, and now they can take a cure back to their village. The primordial race of Tree People have more than their share of Old Time doctors. Tippy digs through the dirt and uncovers the medicine, and Tommy carefully places it into his backpack.

Tommy and Tippy wait for the rain to let up. As the trees drip their last drops, sunshine streams through the grove. They race back through the woods and triumphantly rejoin the others. Their world has been saved.

I walk deeper into the grove. Midday sunlight streams down, picks up the green of the redwood limbs and gives the grove a pastel look of primal holiness. I sit in this light until my own breathing joins the breath of the trees and I feel part of the green calm of this ancient forest.

Though the ocean is not far off, I don't hear the hissing of the surf, nor do I hear traffic from the highway. The thickness of the grove muffles outside noises and creates an amphitheater for smaller sounds within its hearing: the trickling of a creek, squirrels scurrying through the undergrowth, the songs of birds, and, below the soil, a deep groan from the depths. I imagine I hear redwood roots slowly stretching and pushing the trees higher and higher.

Also contained within the grove is the weather. Like lofty mountain peaks, these tall trees reshape sunlight and clouds into patterns uniquely their own. Light struggles to filter through the thick branches of the trees. By the time it reaches the forest floor, it has fractured into many spots of light, some lighting the trunks of trees, some the dark-green ferns and carpets of clover, some sending light deep into pools in the creek.

Likewise, large banks of clouds are split into pockets of fog and mist as they settle into the grove, adding moisture to the soil and droplets to the broad leaves of a diversity of rainforest plants. The redwoods drink up much of this moisture, eventually giving it back to the grove in a self-created gentle rain.

The thickest groves lack the undergrowth of other trees and plants that show the seasons. Here the redwoods control the weather to such an extreme that no particular season is apparent. A scene of fog and damp ferns, a trickling creek, the reddish bark and green boughs of the trees ... this scene might be a day in January or its twin in July.

This existence outside our rules of time gives each grove an ageless aura. I imagine how things looked on the first morning of Mythtime. Did the beginnings of our oldest stories have the same light and texture as I now experience in this forest? I let my imagination explore. I whisper the first word of an old myth, and the sound feels at home in this grove.

This quiet time in the trees doesn't last long. A canine interruption of everything sacred appears out of nowhere. In a theatrical hiatus of self-applauding wolf whistles and howls, Mister Coyote enters and plays all of his roles. He is the Creator's truth-making Fool, a hot-headed doggy demagogue, a canine rabble-rouser, a self-styled spiritual advisor, the master tale teller of all Mythtime. He swaggers into the heart of the trees and poses at the bottom of a shaft of sunshine like a vainglorious pup of an actor in his spotlight. He extends a paw, makes a satire of a sweeping Shakespearean gesture, and narrows it at me. Coyote's voice is made dramatic by its raspy whisper.

"Having a little New Age moment, are we?"

"What do you mean?"

"Don't forget, Mister Native Storyteller. Each New Age is a shadow of an older age."

"I see. Care to elaborate?"

"Of course! You're wise to ask the expert. I am the shining star of the Old Time stories. I was here at the beginning, and I'm still here. Most of the footprints around the First Redwood are my paw prints. Me and the Creator have been buddies for a long time."

"Just what did you do in this neck of the woods?"

"For one thing, I stole fire and gave it to the people. I hid the power of fire in the redwoods. That's why redwoods have thick bark. They are keepers of the fire, by my permission, of course."

"Of course. Anything else?"

"I know all the Old Time people who live around here: the giant serpents who nap in the lakes and use submerged redwoods for pillows, and monsters and dark ghosts who give you humans the willies, and the heroes of the stories—Raven, Bear, Eagle. The heroes are me in disguise, you know. I have a large collection of masks. There are more stories about me in the redwoods than you can ever imagine."

"Since you know everything, have you heard the story of the two-headed monster?"

"What a silly question! I was there when the four brothers fought the monster. When that two-mouthed, truth-twisting, two-timing monster walked through the redwoods, he was the pounding wind of a fierce storm. Branches broke off everywhere he went, and entire trees toppled and crashed to the ground. The world shook with every step he took. He killed three of the brothers, but the fourth, the youngest, succeeded in slaying the monster. I would have killed him myself if I hadn't been delayed in another story. But I got there in time to see the final battle."

"Where did this happen?"

"Not far from here. Monsters are never far away."

"Have you been there lately?"

"Some of us have the courage to visit places where evil forces destroy people and level the giant trees. Others I know play it safe and hang out in the old growth, meditating, concocting coyote-less chants, embracing ancient trees, and happily feeling part of something universally sacred, moderately shallow, and obviously obscure. Personally, I prefer to experience the entire story."

"Okay, Mister Dog, you're pouring it on pretty thick. What are you getting at?"

"Who, me?"

"Yes, you. What's up?"

"Want a challenge? Something with depth in your New Age? Want to experience the pawnote to all the Old Time stories you've been studying? Want to be a storyteller with qualifications?"

"What do you have in mind?"

"Take a little walk. Have a look at the clearcut beyond these trees. Just make sure you search deep for those stories that matter."

"What will I find?"

"The truths of trees."

"In the absence of trees?"

"You harebrained human! You have trouble interpreting your own gut feelings. Not even the logger who felled those giants ate his lunch in the cut. He went back into the trees where it's shady and comfortable."

"What's that got to do with stories?"

"Must I always explain everything about stories to the so-called storyteller? Well, listen up. You might learn something. When the youngest brother killed the two-headed monster, the monster limped away from the downed trees, deep into the living forest to gasp his last breath. At the end of his life, he was drawn to his roots. In addition, if I hadn't been there and had a look at things, I wouldn't be able to tell the story as it happened. The story would have been lost."

"What about the youngest brother? Didn't he tell the story?"

"Not with my artistic flair, and he lacked my astute powers of observation, not to mention my ability to shapeshift between worlds. There's something to be said for tellers who have first-hand experiences with their stories."

"It's more difficult to find Old Time stories these days."

"Not for those with their eyes open."

"What would you have me do?"

"Wander between worlds. Take a walk out of the trees. Visit the battlefield and confront the monster. Time might have altered the monster, but it hasn't changed his story. It still lingers there. Perhaps you're scared to leave the coziness of your unscathed womb of the woods."

Coyote stands tall in the sunlight. He takes several bows, applauds himself, and waves to the trees. He knows when to exit. He howls and laughs as he scampers off his self-made stage. He disappears into the shadows. Coyote never repeats a curtain call.

I think things through. As much as I hesitate to admit it, Coyote's foolish talk is woven with wisdom. I draw a deep breath in the trees. I grip Coyote's challenge. I walk out of the grove and into the devastation of a coastal clearcut.

Twilight softens the view with gentle light and long shadows. At this time between day and night, the path to Mythtime becomes visible. I imagine centuries of storytellers sharing their stories here where the trees once stood. I imagine the laughter of children as they listen to tales that dramatize the many antics of clever Coyote. I hear friendly arguments among their parents, "Which are older? The trees or the stories?" An elder answers, "They're the same age. They're twins. They came into the world together."

This clearcut might be a graveyard for trees and stories, but where the dead are, their ghosts live. Though the stories are fractured, there are whispers of monologues that rise out of stumps and dialogues that speak through heaps of broken branches. Echoes of entire stories swirl like fog over a bare hillside of newly planted seedlings, as if trying to wake them up and make them grow.

Standing on the edge, I clearly hear the most recent native story, which is also the most ominous. When she was 102 years old, Chilula elder and religious leader Minnie Reeves warned us of this moment.

"The redwood trees are sacred. They are a special gift and reminder from the Great Creator to the human beings. The Great Creator made everything, including trees of all kinds, but he wanted to leave a special gift for his children. So he took a little medicine from each tree, he said a prayer and sang a powerful song, and then he mixed it all with the blood of our people. Then he created this special redwood tree from his medicine. He left it on Earth as a demonstration of his love for his children. The redwood trees have a lot of power: they are the tallest, live the longest, and are the most beautiful trees in the world. Destroy these trees and you destroy the Creator's love. And if you destroy that which the Creator loves so much, you will eventually destroy mankind."

I sit all night on a log on the edge between the grove and the clearcut. I listen to the footsteps of animals, the breath of the wind as it sweeps up from the coast and intermingles with the trees, the deep night filled with the wisdom of silence. Beyond the silence I hear voices of trees whispering their truths.

There is little light at sunrise. Clouds roll in from the ocean and dim the first light of the day. Fall colors look pale. Here is the faded photograph of my childhood with a new lure. I look past the picture frame and know I have more journeys to make. Through the long, dark winter ahead, I'll return and share the traditional stories. Someone should speak them here or they'll be forgotten. I'll listen to the landscape, learn the newest stories, and share them, as well. In the spring sunshine, from the edge of the grove, I'll watch the seedlings grow. In the company of stories, I'll welcome them home.

THE LEGEND OF TABLE MOUNTAIN

For several years a legend has sauntered around the rugged Greensprings country of southern Oregon. Like all good legends, it grows as it sloshes through creeks and rivers, traipses into canyons, and wanders deep into the shadows of old-growth forests. Eventually the legend clambers up a steep ridge to the towering height of a mountain peak. If the legend survives the climb, it finds a mythic place in the landscape and in the hearts of people who call the Greensprings their home.

This legend tells of an old man who spends his winters in the abandoned fire lookout on the summit of Table Mountain. Like an ancient character in a many-layered story, he is many images woven into one: the wise man on the mountain peak, the hermit in the forest chapel, a monk in his cell studying texts, an elder with a vivid memory of the Old Time stories and how things used to be, the old man who abandoned the weight of the world to search in the wilderness for the song of his heart ...

The story says that before he came to Table Mountain, the man traveled nearly every day of his life. As an anthropologist and linguist, he was obsessed with saving native cultures—myths, languages, folklore, history, songs—and he scribbled nearly every word ever spoken to him. He filled notebook after notebook with observations, insights, and shreds of folklore and language. He stashed hundreds of boxes of notes in "safe" places to be retrieved at a later time, when something might be done with the raw data. He put what little money he earned into second-hand clothes, fuel for his rig, and into notebooks and pencils.

As years went by, his obsession to collect cultures never slowed. He rarely enjoyed his travels or noticed much of the world as it breezed by him. There was too much to be done. Ancient civilizations were being lost, and quickly. Those moments between native informants were shadowed with the worries and troubled dreams of a riveted urgency. As years went by, he forgot where the notebooks had been stashed.

Each time he traveled to a new interview, he was certain that a dozen informants were dying at that very moment—perhaps the last speakers of their native languages—and he would never be able to record their stories. They would be lost to the world forever. Once he had a friend run over his legs with a car to keep him out of the army so he could continue working. Another time he gave a dying informant morphine to keep him alive a little longer, long enough to scribble another story and a few more words from a dying language.

More years went by. He grew old. His clothes wore thin. Even on the hottest days he wore a threadbare jacket to hide his shirt that was split up the back. His rig labored and chugged with each trip. He tried to keep up the pace of his youth, but he was tired. The old man slowed down.

One fall morning, as he sat exhausted, he looked away from his field notes and noticed a mountain peak brushed white with a light dusting of new snow. It was beautiful. The longer he gazed at the mountain, the less tired he felt. He put his field notes on the ground. His felt light, unburdened. At that moment he replaced his obsession with a new horizon. He let go of everyone else's stories and began to think about his own.

He stored his field notes in his memory, left behind his rig, and slowly made his way to the summit of the mountain. He climbed the rickety steps to the top of the old fire lookout and looked out upon the world. He tossed away his mental debris and began to contemplate what was left of his life, his own place in the great story of the world.

As winter neared, the old man gathered firewood, got the stove working, carried in food and water, fuel for a lantern, and repaired the old cot and heaped it with blankets. As snowdrifts closed the roads and trails, he gazed upon the landscape where he had spent his life, and everything looked foreign.

All winter, during the storytelling season of long nights, his mind traveled through every story he had ever heard. As though stories were as real as the landscape, he put himself into each narrative and began to experience each story as if he were there. As he traveled through stories, he traveled through seasons and watched the landscape evolve as each story changed.

In the spring, he walked down the mountain and discovered the relationship between stories and walking: the rhythm and pace of the story, the measured feet of the poetry of the language, each step shuffling through story and landscape, the silence between the words and between each breath of the warm breeze. He spoke new versions of the stories as he walked. The earth warmed, trees leafed out, spring sunlight pushed away the shadows of winter. With each word of each story, with his own presence as the storyteller, the old man recreated his world as spring remakes winter with the warm-hearted telling of its arrival.

The old man walked through shifting storyscapes of spring and summer and into the fall. He never felt alone. His companions were stories and the places where they continue to thrive. Before the first snow, he returned to Table Mountain for another winter of contemplation and story making.

He remembered that he had first come to the mountain with the Takelma elder Gwisgwashan. It was a November day, ages ago. He was on one of his many ethnographic field trips. But this time he returned not as a collector of stories, but as a story himself.

He became a legend. Perhaps someday he'll become a myth. He soon forgot those fixated field trips of his former life. He forgot his troubled dreams and worries. He even forgot his name. What he remembers are the stories, which are the summit of his life. As he looks out from the lookout, he opens his eyes wide and the landscape feels like home.

The story says that he has few visitors. He is gone on his walks for most of the year, and when snow closes the mountain roads, he is cut off from the rest of the world. He is alone in his snowy lookout, spinning and re-spinning tales in the shadows of the long nights and in the warm glow of lantern light and firelight. Every so often, someone journeys through the mountain snow and finds the old man in his lookout. The old man tells one of his stories, and the visitor takes the story home, where it is told again and again. A few folks have come across the old man on his walks, and, likewise, they are each given a story to take home. The stories are not lost after all.

This legend is about many things, and so it is destined for a long life. It has been written as it has been told, season after season. The facts shift from version to version, but the truths of the legend never falter and remain unchanged as the legend continues to grow.

JACKRABBIT CUTS DOWN TREES

On Table Mountain, an old man tells this story.

Just down the ridge is Cottonwood Glades, one of the battlegrounds of the first war. It's a peaceful place now, a far cry from the bloody shrieks that echoed across this land those many centuries ago. The path of that war snaked through this entire region, from one knife-in-belly battle site to the next, from the sacred banks of the river, along the creeks, high into the hills, eventually slithering back to the river. And for what? Misunderstanding, misinformation, and an outrage upon the land. The story may be old, but the truths of it live with us now.

In the time we call the Old Time, when animals and people were not so different, the time of myths, of dreams, when the landscape stretched beyond sight, when trees were so plentiful it seemed they would last forever, at such a time as this, the people tell a story about Jackrabbit, Coyote, the people, and the people's relations, the trees.

Wili yowo. There was a house along the river, and Jackrabbit lived by himself in that house, away from the village.

It was fall. Morning fog pressed low on forests of pines and firs and cedars, and oaks and maples blazed yellow and red through the fog as their leaves fell and fell and fell.

The people were gone from the village, scattered through fog to the meadows to dig camas roots for the coming winter. As trees dropped their leaves, the forests lost color. Even evergreens seemed pale in the gray fog. While the people were digging camas, Jackrabbit was alone in his house, away from the village.

Jackrabbit woke with a start and crossed his ears. He looked through the fog toward the village and said to himself, "Where has everyone gone now that camas is ripe?" He jumped out of his house. "So they've gone digging, eh? I'll show them I can be as useful as they are. I can get ready for winter, too. I'll cut firewood."

He grabbed his ax and laid out his ears, hop-hopping into the forest as fast as he could.

"I'll cut enough wood for everyone, enough for a hundred winters!"

Jackrabbit didn't settle for gathering dead, fallen wood. He cut down live trees. He cut pine trees, which give the people planks and beams for their houses. He cut oak trees, the sons and daughters of Acorn Woman who provides food. He even cut the medicine trees, whose bark and sap and leaves keep the people healthy. He cut every tree in sight. He worked in a frenzy, cutting trees still brilliant in their fall colors.

He hacked and he hacked, and each time he stopped to catch his breath, he crossed his ears, and with a fevered look in his eyes, he said to himself, "I'm so good at this. If it was anyone else, the trees would fall on top of him. But not me. I'm a useful Jackrabbit. A talented Jackrabbit. The people's provider! I'm the … But what am I saying? I should be cutting. These trees are as ripe as camas."

He cut trees all day. He hacked and he hacked, and the trees fell and fell and fell. And the fog pressed lower.

Day settled into shadows as the people returned to the village, their baskets brimmed with camas roots. Coyote, his nose tuned to thoughts of a full belly, was padding through fog along the river when he heard Jackrabbit hacking down trees. "Hmmmmm. Interesting."

Coyote stopped. He put an ear to the ground and heard Jackrabbit talking to himself: "I'm the best hacker there is. When I cut them all down, I'll dump them in the river and float them to the village. I'll show the people I'm as good as they are! But what am I saying? Time to be cutting!"

Coyote turned his nose to the village, carrying his version of the news to the people.

When he got there he said, "There's a fuzzy bunny upriver killing your relations. He hacks them in two and dumps their bodies in the river. I heard him say so himself."

Word got around, and everyone gathered in the dance house. Thinking that Jackrabbit was killing their human relations, they tied their hair into topknots. They dusted their foreheads with white paint. They prepared for the first war there ever was. They grabbed their spears. One by one through the night and the fog, the people followed Coyote upriver, into the woods.

One man found Jackrabbit, and Coyote told him, "That's the one I told you about."

But the man replied, "That one? You've got to be kidding. He's too small. He would make a plaything for my child." The man scooped Jackrabbit into a basket and fell in at the back of the line.

Jackrabbit coiled his legs, made a great leap out of the basket, and hop-hopped back into the woods. But nobody noticed. They were all looking ahead, walking in a long line upriver, looking for the one who was killing their relations.

Another man found Jackrabbit, and Coyote said, "That's the one who's been killing people. That's the one!"

But the man said, "No, no. You must have it wrong. That one looks like a toy for my child." He stuffed Jackrabbit into a basket and joined the first man at the back of the line. Again, without anyone noticing, Jackrabbit leaped out and disappeared into the woods.

How many times did they find Jackrabbit, and how many times was Coyote not believed? Through the night, along the river, through the fog, many of them found Jackrabbit. But each time, he escaped.

It was only when the people got together back at the village that they realized they had been catching the same rabbit. "What did yours look like?" "Furry, with long ears." "That's the one I caught. But he got away." "So did mine." "Mine, too."

At this point someone suggested that Coyote might be telling the truth.

"If that little rabbit could escape so many times, I suppose he could kill our relations." Everyone agreed to go after Jackrabbit again in the morning. They went to bed with thoughts that led to uncomfortable dreams.

Next morning, the people gathered and again prepared for war. Coyote joined them, and they started upriver toward the last place they had seen Jackrabbit.

It wasn't hard to find him. In the daylight they could see the trees cut down, and they followed the path of Jackrabbit's cutting.

Some trees had fallen over others. Some lay half in the river. Nothing was left alive. No trees. No bushes. No plants. Jackrabbit had hacked everything to the ground.

The people froze.

Eyes widened. Brows lowered. Anger fired their eyes.

Jackrabbit stuck his ears into the air like war feathers and looked to where the people stood, dead still. "Ahhhhh, more trees? Just when anyone else would have thought the job was done, Jackrabbit sees more trees." He grabbed his ax, rushed the people, and cut several through. They fell among the stumps and cut-through trunks of the sons and daughters of Acorn Woman, the pines, the firs, the cedars and all the other trees. They fell and fell and fell.

With a swiftness that surprised himself, Coyote grabbed the ax and cut Jackrabbit to the ground. He hacked him to pieces and tossed him into the river.

Somewhere a lark started singing. The morning breeze picked up the song and carried it downriver toward the village. Then there was silence, as filling as night.

The few survivors walked back to the village. They spent the winter mourning the dead and telling and retelling the story of Jackrabbit. Snow buried the stumps and logs until they were vivid only in the memories of the people.

The days were crisp and clear in the spring. Coyote had taken up hunting rabbits. Camas bloomed in the meadows. Wildflowers blazed yellow and red along the riverbanks, and between stumps and rotting logs new saplings took root.

It took many years for new trees to smooth the scars of Jackrabbit's work. Every winter the people gathered around a fire in the dance house and told the story. "As long as the story lives, the trees will live," says the storyteller. "If the story dies, that will be the end of us and the end of our relations, the trees."

SIXTH GRADE AND BEYOND

WHEN I WAS IN THE SIXTH GRADE, I had a math teacher who seated us in the classroom according to what grade we got on the last test. There was an A row, a B row, a C row, and, of course, a D row and an F row. Being a future artist and not very good at math, I was always in one of the last two rows.

That same year, I had a writing teacher I adored. She was a wonderful woman. One day she took me aside and said, "Tommy, you do pretty well with words." She got a glimmer in her eye. "I bet if you worked harder on your writing and got better at it, it would matter to you less which row you sat in in math."

That was a revelation for me. And that day—in sixth grade—I decided to become a writer. I also became a listener and a watcher of things. I was the kid on the playground who always stood back from the crowd, and I listened and I watched. I took it all in: the sounds of the play-ground—the laughter, the shouting, the crying—and the way things looked: how the sunlight slanted down, how clouds rode on the wind. I began to write stories and poems about what I heard and what I saw.

Years later, when I decided to become a storyteller, I told my ninety-year-old grandpa. He considered this, and then his eyes started shining. "That's good," he said. "You never were very good at math. Just make sure you know how to figure so you don't get done over!"

At first I thought he meant to make sure I charge enough money when I tell stories. But as I dove into the stories, I began to understand how deeply stories affect us and how long they stay with us. Bit by bit, I figured out that Grandpa was referring to much more than money.

These days I'm still a listener and a watcher of things. That's how I get stories. By spending time in the magical places the stories come from, by listening to the language of the landscape, by listening to wise people tell their stories. By paying attention to the details.

I eventually returned to my elementary school as a storyteller, and the only teacher still there from when I was a student was the math teacher! I went into the school office to introduce myself to the principal, and the secretary said, "Mr. Doty, have a seat. She'll be right with you." I plopped down in an ancient oak chair and began to feel uncomfortable. I had spent plenty of time in this same office as a student, and this was probably the same chair I used to squirm in. I glanced through the window into the principal's office and recognized the scene. The principal was talking seriously to a young boy. Neither of them looked happy. And then I laughed to myself. Not much has changed, I thought. Here I am, sitting in the office waiting to see the principal and thinking about which stories I'm going to tell. But this time, I'm getting paid to be here.

Grandpa would be proud—proud of the paycheck—and so much more.

THE WIND

THE WIND IS THE BREATH OF THE earth. To take a deep breath and slowly exhale is to imitate creation and give long life not only to yourself, but to everything around you: trees and soil, fog and clouds, sun, moon and stars, creeks and rivers that tumble and twist and feel the breeze as it ties the woods together.

The wind blew when Children Maker breathed fog and made the world, when Coyote, trickster of a thousand myths, walked up and down the rivers and creeks, shaping the landscape.

The wind blew when the first storyteller moved breath into words and told stories as winter storms screamed through the village. The stories taught the people to sing forgiveness to the deer before the hunt, to call trees their relations, to celebrate the aliveness of their world.

The wind blew when roads swallowed the trails, when deer hid from a different kind of hunter, when the rip of saws cleared whole families of forests.

The wind still blows. It is the breath of the earth, the music of the shaking leaves, the primal teller of all stories.

The wind keeps the world going.

A MYTHTIME WALK UP LOWER TABLE ROCK

IN OUR TAKELMA LANGUAGE, WILI YOWO MEANS "there was a house." These words, like the first steps of a journey, begin every Takelma myth.

Though many of Takelmas are gone from their Rogue Valley world, our myths live on in the landscape of our homeland: in the thunder of the river, the hooting of owls on the Table Rocks, the movements of the sun and moon.

I recently took my own journey into the center of our myths, from the Rogue River up the old Indian trail to the top of Lower Table Rock. Spanning sunrise to sunrise, this journey became a story in itself. Everything I had learned about the myths became a personal experience, coming alive as I walked into the heart of where stories come from.

Wili yowo. There was a house along the Rogue River. There were many Old Time houses wrapped in a village. Morning sunlight slanted across their rooftops, drifting down smoke holes, the way it now skims the surface of the river and dives into its depths.

We call this river Gelam. It flows east to west as it has done since anyone can remember. In the myths, there are two directions: upriver and downriver. Upriver is to the east, toward the rising sun, toward creation. Downriver is to the west, toward the setting sun and the Land of the Dead. If you ask Coyote how to get to the Land of the Dead, he'll tell you, "It's to the west, beyond the sunset, across the river, always on the other side from where I am." This river is a symbol of birth and life and death.

It seems fitting that my own journey should begin here, as any journey into myth is also a journey into symbols. For thousands of years native stories have traveled upriver and downriver, from village to village, breaths of words now riding the west wind, now the east wind, now swirling like fog over Lower Table Rock.

I start up the trail from the river through woods so thick it seems like twilight all the time. Behind me are sunlit meadows of camas and Indian plums and wild carrots, and the river swelled with salmon and sunlight. Morning shadows move like thunderheads through these woods. Voles tunnel under madrone leaves with a whisper and a crackle as if expecting a storm. Woodrats scamper into their nests of heaped-up twigs. Bones along the trail remind me that in these woods there is death as well as life.

Looking back, I no longer see the river, only shadows. I imagine all the monsters Takelmas have seen in the smoke and haze, in the blur of fall wind, in the frozen stillness of winter.

These woods seem long and dark, like a winter night. I see oak leaves floating downriver. Oak trees push up like skeletons against the night. The cold moon moves across the sky, the same color as ice along the edge of the river before the sun rises up. Mist moves through these woods, rolls along the river.

Now is the time of hoot owls in the darkness, calling death and stealing children. Bad-hearted shamans cause sickness in people they don't like. Rolling skulls of dead people kill everyone they roll over. The river serpent squeezes people to death.

Now is the spirit time of dark nights. Fall wind swirls mist and fog over and over the burial mounds. The wind cries to the dead ones, far into winter.

I imagine I am inside a winter lodge, the storm howling down the smoke hole. A storyteller moves through smoke and shadows, his movement now slow like the purr of the fire, now wild with the storm.

These are his words.

◇◇◇◇◇

Wili yowo. It had been cold for a long time. The Rogue River froze over, and the snow fell and fell, making drifts all through the valley.

Coyote and Roasting Dead People lived along the river, each in his own house, each with a child. They were neighbors.

Snow drifted over the tops of their houses. They hadn't been able to go outside for days. They were running out of food, and Roasting Dead People's child was nearly dead from hunger.

Days went by, days went by, days went by …

The cold didn't let up. The entire world was snow and ice, and there was no food anywhere. And one morning, just as the weather broke, the child of Roasting Dead People died.

Roasting Dead People pushed on the door to his house, but it wouldn't open. He had to push hard to break open the door through the shell of ice that covered the house. He went next door and said to Coyote, "Say, Coyote, my friend. My child has died. Will you lend me a blanket so I can bury him properly?"

Coyote was annoyed. He yelled from inside his house, "Don't bother me! Don't you know that if you bury your child with a blanket he'll come back around this place? What's going to happen if dead people come back around here?"

So Roasting Dead People went home and buried his child without a blanket.

Days went by, days went by …

Winter turned into spring, which moved into summer, and fall brought the cold days again. When winter came, it was the coldest anyone could remember. The Rogue River froze over again. Snow piled high, and food was running short. And one morning, as clouds pulled apart and the sun started shining, Coyote's child got sick and died.

Coyote went next door and said to Roasting Dead People, "Give me a blanket. My child's kicked off, and I've got to bury the kid."

Roasting Dead People couldn't believe what he was hearing. "What's that you're saying? A year ago when I asked you the same thing, all you could say was, 'What's going to happen if dead people come back?' Now my child is rotting!"

Coyote went home and buried his child.

Days went by …

Coyote sat in the doorway to his house and watched winter turn into spring. Ice in the river melted away. Wildflowers started blooming along the riverbanks. And Coyote kept saying to himself, "People are never coming back after they die. Not ever, my child, not ever."

Now this part of the story is finished, says the storyteller. Go gather seeds and eat them.

Sunlight rushes through me like summer wind. I move out of the woods, to where the trail hugs the lower bones of the cliff, and up and up and onto the top of Lower Table Rock.

Midday heat is intense. Heat waves, like the wind, shimmer above summer-brown grasses. Voles are quiet in their cool, damp tunnels under mounds of earth. Rattlesnakes doze in the shadows. I walk across the rock to the best shade around: the cedar trees.

Wind hits my face. I watch vultures and eagles ride thermals out of the bowl and across the rock, then along the eastern cliff across the top and back into the bowl. Vultures circle low just to make sure I'm moving. Eagles watch from the heights of clouds. The wind is hot and dry, making sure I know it's summer.

We tell a story of a terrible drought. The river was so low there weren't any salmon to catch. Leaves fell off trees long before fall. There weren't any berries in the mountains. No water. No breeze to cool the air. Nothing but stale, stagnant heat.

They hired a fellow to make rain. He climbed to the top of the rock and turned on the rain. But he never turned it off. The river swelled to a lake that covered the entire Takelma world.

The man changed into a cedar tree, safe on the rock above the water. His son and his son's wife and their little boy fled the valley to join him, turning into rock pinnacles that jutted over the flood. Entire villages washed away, and many Takelmas drowned.

Angry survivors hired Beaver to chew down the rock. He chewed and he chewed, but when it occurred to him that he might get squashed by the falling rock, he quit. You can still see his teeth marks near the base of the cliff.

The first thing the people knew of the world returning to normal was the summer wind, a warm wind that stopped the rain and sent the river back within its banks. The people survived. But they never forgot the terror of the drought and the flood. And they never forgot the wind.

It feels good to sit in the shade of the cedar out of the midday heat and to feel the wind move across the rock, clearing the air.

The Old Ones have a medicine poem they say to the wind:

"Hey! From the lower part of my body you will drive away evil things bad. From the crown of my head you will drive them away. From over my hands you will drive them away. From within my backbone you will drive away evil things bad. From above my feet you will drive away evil things bad. OOOOO!" (The people blow to the wind.)

Almost sunset. I sit on the edge of the rock. I look east toward the beginning of the river, away from the Land of the Dead, here on Lower Table Rock, on the back of Younger Daldal, giant dragonfly and Takelma culture bringer. Along with his elder brother, nearby Upper Table Rock, he decided to stop here and live his life after their great journey up the Rogue River from the coast, changing things and making the world right.

The sun sets behind me. Stars open up. I close my eyes and imagine myself in an Old Time sweat house, dripping water on hot rocks, steam rising around me, getting hotter and hotter.

My head nearly bursts with heat. Stars shoot through the steam. A tunnel opens in the dirt floor.

I crawl down the tunnel, through the rock, and I hear the timbers of the sweat house creak as they shake with heat. Crawling toward the river, the creaking of the timbers becomes the creaking of the bones of generations of Takelmas, the entire rock shaking under their burial mounds. There is a faint light as I crawl out the end of the tunnel, toward the thunder of the river.

I sit on the riverbank, back at the beginning of the trail. The sun sends morning light across the river, and not long after, a sliver of new moon rises and moves with the sun across the sky. I sit and I listen, and I hear voices seep through cracks in the rock, voices from another time, yet still strong today. The voices rise with the rising of the new moon.

"I shall prosper, still longer I shall go. Even people, if they say of me, I wish you were dead. You! Just like I shall do, again I shall rise. Even many beings, when they devour you. Frogs, when they eat you up. Many beings, little snakes banded. Even those when they eat you, still again do you rise. You! Just like I shall do in time to come! BO!" (They yell and they yell and they yell.)

I'm thinking that as surely as the moon shall rise again and again, I will climb this rock many more times. I shall again journey into our mythic world, into stories that teach me the dignity of death and the beauty of being alive.

Takelma myths have a traditional ending, "Gweldi. Baybit leplap," which means "Finished! Now go collect seeds and eat them." In other words you've been sitting around listening to stories long enough, so get up and go gather food. Now that you've gathered seeds of wisdom from the stories, it's time to gather seeds for nourishment. Both kinds of seeds are necessary for the survival of humankind. Without food, there is no life. Without myths, life has no meaning.

PANTHER AND THE DEER

In the winter lodges, the people tell this story.

Panther and his younger brother Wildcat lived along the Rogue River. Deep into fall, the oak trees were nearly bare of their leaves. Panther hunted every day and brought home many deer. They had more meat than they could eat, so they ate the best pieces and let the rest rot. Though it was nearly winter, they didn't dry any meat to store. They ate what they wanted and the rest spoiled. Panther hunted until the deer were as few as the leaves on the oak trees.

The few remaining deer gathered in their mountain cave. "Panther is killing us off. We must do something." They sent him a deer girl to marry.

Panther didn't know she was a deer. She covered herself with a blanket and kept to the shadows, back from the fire. From that day on, Panther found no more deer. He hunted morning to night, and he always came home empty handed.

Days got colder. Oak trees were skeletons, white with frost. There was no more meat in the house. Panther and Wildcat were dead hungry.

Panther's deer wife collected firewood covered with moss and stacked it inside. Next morning the moss was gone.

Panther was weak. His legs barely worked. He muttered, "Where have all the deer gone?" He stumbled along the riverbank, searching and searching.

Wildcat tried to help his brother, but he was also hungry and weak.

Panther's deer wife stacked firewood. One evening, she took out her obsidian knife. She cut two strips of flesh off her own legs and put them into the fire to cook.

Panther and Wildcat came home, full of hunger. "Where have all the deer gone? We almost couldn't get home because we were so hungry."

Panther's deer wife pointed to the fire. The brothers each took a piece of meat. It was roasted, like venison. It was deer meat.

That night, Panther stayed awake, thinking, "Where did she get that meat?"

Outside, the wind screamed through the trees. Clouds slid down the mountains and rolled along the river. The night turned cold, white with blowing snow.

Panther's deer wife got out of bed, thinking, "He is asleep." She crept to the firewood and ate the moss off every piece. That's how she got her food.

While she was eating, Panther watched from the shadows. In the firelight, he saw her legs where they were cut away.

"You are a deer!" Panther grabbed his bow, fitted an arrow, shot at her ... and missed.

Panther's deer wife bounded across the house. She jumped at her husband, slashed his belly with her knife and ripped out his pancreas. In one giant leap she was out the door, carrying Panther's pancreas in her mouth. She disappeared into the blowing snow.

The storm blew away in the morning. The sun shone bright on a snow-covered field near the cave where the deer gathered. Panther's deer wife ran onto the field.

"That is Panther's pancreas!" the deer shouted. One of the deer rushed out and grabbed it.

"Catch up with him, One-Horned Deer!" One-Horned Deer rushed out, grabbed the pancreas, and made long leaps to the other end of the field.

For the rest of the day, the deer played shinny ball under the winter sun, and they used Panther's pancreas for the ball.

All night along the river, Panther lay in a sweat house, losing his spirit. Wildcat sent people, through the snow and night shadows, to steal back his brother's pancreas. Medicine Fawn, a powerful doctor among the deer, danced around the fire, singing her medicine song:

Wa-ya-we-ne lo-wa-na.
Wa-ya-we-ne lo-wa-na.
Wa-ya-we-ne lo-wa-na.

Who creeps there about the shadows?
Who creeps there about the shadows?
Who creeps there about the shadows?

Wa-ya-we-ne lo-wa-na.

She discovered every thief, and the deer chased them out of their cave.

In the morning, Medicine Fawn traveled to the sweat house where Wildcat was watching his brother die. She jumped inside. "Ugly-faced Wildcat, your elder brother calls you 'Crack-bones!' You useless Wildcat, you do-nothing brother!"

That night Wildcat sent more people to steal the pancreas. Medicine Fawn danced and sang her medicine song, and the deer chased them all away.

Wildcat thought, "Maybe she is right. Maybe I'd better do it myself." He gathered moss off the oak trees and stuck it all over his body, even on his hands.

Wildcat went to the shinny ball field. He stood by himself, looking like a clump of moss in the trampled snow. One-Horned Deer ran toward him, carrying Panther's pancreas. When he got close to Wildcat he tossed the pancreas to another deer. Wildcat stretched out his arm, caught it in mid-flight, and took off down the mountains.

"Catch up with him, One-Horned Deer!"

Wildcat ran until he was tired. He climbed a tree, but many deer were close behind. He was surrounded.

The deer used their antlers to uproot the tree. Wildcat leaned on the top so it would fall toward his trail. When the tree hit the snow, Wildcat scampered off and ran ahead of the deer.

"Catch up with him, One-Horned Deer!"

The chase went into the night. Wildcat climbed another tree. Again he was surrounded. But the deer were also tired and decided to rest before uprooting the tree. Soon they were sleeping.

Wildcat put more moss on himself. He crept down. He leapt lightly onto the antlers of the nearest deer, then onto another deer's antlers. He moved across the antlers toward the trail. But as he landed on the last antlers, his leg brushed the face of the sleeping deer and woke him up.

"Catch up with him!"

The deer bounded after Wildcat. He ran through the night, carrying the pancreas, winding through the snowy woods, trying to lose the deer. It was nearly sunrise when he got to the sweat house.

Inside, his brother lay belly up, mostly dead. Wildcat rushed in, tossed his brother's pancreas between his ribs, and Panther jumped up. The deer surrounded the sweat house, snorting and stamping the snow. Both brothers grabbed their bows and started shooting. Panther shot at the large deer and Wildcat at the smaller ones. But all the arrows missed. The arrows sang as they whizzed through the air, "Don't kill too many! Don't kill too many!" And Panther and Wildcat heard their song.

The deer scattered, some into the mountains, some along the river, some down the valley. Through the rest of the winter, Panther and Wildcat hunted together. They killed only what they needed and wasted no meat. They had plenty of food, but never too much.

In the spring, many fawns were born, and the deer were as many as new leaves on the oak trees.

ON YOUNGER DALDAL'S BACK

Coyote and I traipse across the top of the flat-topped mesa called Lower Table Rock. On this autumn night, the stars burn bright and a rosy moon blushes just over the horizon. Tiny red lights flicker along the trail, and larger ones blink in the trees on Upper Table Rock, across the valley. Fog snakes along the valley floor, shrouding the Rogue River and the many communities scattered along its course. But Coyote and I walk between fog and stars, and the night breathes mystery into our hearts.

Coyote says, "This is just the sort of night we might meet him."

"Him?"

"Yes, him, that ancient one, the master of tricksters from the Old Time, that younger dragonfly brother. Across the valley there, that's Elder Daldal, the older of the two brothers. He's far too serious to my liking. But here on this rock, we are standing on the back of Younger Daldal, master of tricks and magic and brimming with humor. We are standing right on him."

We walk on, crossing the abandoned landing strip, stepping carefully between ankle-twisting rocks, sloshing through vernal pools circled by rabbitbrush, and finally into the trees. We are getting closer to the edge of the rock, a three-hundred-foot drop onto heaped-up piles of razor-sharp basalt. We feel a damp breeze rush our way from the edge, a breeze that lifts fog from the river and laps it over the top like ocean waves onto a beach.

We pass an ancient black oak twisted with shadows and age. An owl hoots five times. Stars spin. Red lights flash. And before Coyote and I know time has passed, we find ourselves walking dangerously close to the edge, many yards from our last steps, the fog lapping our faces damp.

"That was the younger dragonfly," says Coyote. "See how he works, full of power, the guardian of this rock."

"He might have sent us over the edge. Every few years I hear about someone falling."

"But he didn't," chuckles Coyote. "But he didn't."

Between fog and stars, Coyote and I walk back toward the trail that winds down the rock. Neither of us offers a rational explanation for what has happened. Neither speaks. Each senses that silence is what makes the most sense ... right now ... in such a place as this.

RIBS OF THE ANIMAL

AT HOME IN THE SISKIYOU MOUNTAINS, I am knee-deep in my manuscripts in the upstairs library. I read out loud to myself.

"Through the eyes of the Takelma people, the Earth's body is a great animal. The neck is to the east at Boundary Springs, the ribs alongside the Rogue River at the Table Rocks, and the tail at Gold Beach where the river flows into the ocean. The river is this animal's lifeblood, pulsing and throbbing through the Takelma world.

"Hmmm ... I know there's more pages of this story around here somewhere."

Coyote wanders down the hallway and pokes his nose in. He gazes through the library window and gestures at the expansive view of the Rogue Valley.

"The world's out there, Mister Storyteller, and so are the stories. Libraries. Humph!"

That gives me an idea. I disappear into a closet. I push a few boxes aside. From the back I lift a dust-covered buckskin bag and hold it front of Coyote's curious nose.

"Isn't this your bag of masks?" I ask.

"Perhaps."

"I haven't seen you wearing them for quite a spell."

Coyote smirks. "I don't need them anymore."

"How so?"

"Let's just say that I have embraced my inner spirit pup and I now shapeshift without the aid of external doodads. I am the master shapeshifter of Mythtime and a much-admired powerful pooch without props. I do it all! This comes from spending time outside in the sunshine and not in libraries."

"Right. Well, since you're not using them, do you mind if I borrow your masks?"

"Not at all. But I should warn you. They aren't your usual human-carved, flimsy-facade masks. They are old, carved in a ceremonial way, and they have magic."

"Magic? Not a typical bag of Coyote tricks?"

"You'll see. Mind if I tag along? This might be entertaining."

"No problem," I say.

"So you say," says Coyote.

"Right again."

Through the course of a year, I take Coyote's buckskin bag of magical masks on several treks down the valley to the Table Rocks along the Rogue River ... the Ribs of the Animal ... the heart of our Takelma universe.

The Rock People mask is the oldest mask in the bag. It is gray and brown and the eyes are large, as if they have been open for a long time and have witnessed many amazing and profound events. The stories of the Rock People are so old that they survive in fragments. Some of these fragments are echoes of the first tellers. The memories of their stories are carved and painted on boulders and cliff faces. Before the Table Rocks stood at this place, their Rock ancestors lived here at Dat'gayawada, Alongside the Earth's Ribs.

I put on the Rock People mask and walk slowly along the river. I look through the ancient eyeholes and feel as if I have journeyed into the first days of Mythtime.

"The Rock People are here," I whisper to myself.

In the spring sunshine, I walk the old Indian trail along the river. New grass has grown up along the banks, and oak trees are green with new leaves. Across the river, plum blossoms are thick on branches that hang over the water. The river flows gray-green with snowmelt.

In the middle is an ancient rock with its top sticking out of the riffles. A black otter-like animal slips out of the water, climbs to the top of the rock, and looks around. He notices me, dives back in, and disappears below the surface. This is one of the Old Time healing animals, the first neighbors of the Rock People. Centuries later, when the whites showed up, these animals slipped into the deepest shadows of the ancient world and are rarely seen these days.

I walk downriver past the long lake where two spotted magical dogs live in their stone house. They come out and bark at me as I walk by, friendly woofs that acknowledge me as an old friend.

"Must be the mask," I say to myself.

I walk past places in the myths. Coyote lives here with his wife, Crane. Their daughter gave birth to Rock Boy, one of the Rock People. Some of his relations are healers. Farther along the trail, in the shadow of Sexton Mountain, lives Rock Old Woman. She watches over her people, attends to their needs, and keeps them healthy. People who pass by thank her for their good health.

I remove the mask and walk back along the trail. I see the world as it is now. The lake is dry. The rock in the river has shifted and leans against the riverbank. The Table Rocks are here, and this is good, but power lines wrap around their bases as if holding them together. The few healers who still live at the center of the world seldom show themselves. Not far away, the remains of Rock Old Woman lie buried under the asphalt lanes of Interstate 5.

I am thinking that there must be more to this world than good things gone bad. There are many ways of looking at the landscape. I am determined to try them all until I discover a path that allows me to walk between ancient and modern worlds, and share stories from both.

The Great Animal mask is not what it first appears to be. The eyeholes and mouth seem open but are covered on the inside. The mask wearer cannot see or talk. The ears are open, however, and anyone who wears the mask has exceptional hearing. There are stories that the mask changes colors as the seasons shift. It is an ancient tradition for the mask wearer to sit in the heart of the world and listen to the language of the landscape.

On a hot summer day, I arrive at the Ribs of the Animal. I take the mask of the Great Animal from the bag. It has many colors: sky-blue, leaf-green and the pale brown of summer-dried valley fields and hillsides. Wearing the mask, I sit quietly by the river for a long time. This mask makes its own darkness. Not even brilliant sunlight finds its way in. The mask forces me to listen in the old way of listening to stories. I look inside my mind, grasping some mental image of mythic memory. I imagine story characters in the firelight and shadows of the dance house, moving to the words of the storyteller. I look beyond the dance and see the Great Animal that is the world. I listen to the voice of Mother Landscape tell the first story of this place.

We begin along the Rogue River. Gelam. Here live the People of the River. Takelma. In a house. Wili yowo. Here I speak the words. Here the story begins.

There is something ancient about a beginning, floating in the depths of human memory, a secret the oldest stories recall, a myth the river tells over and over. The beginning is a long time ago that is now.

Our world is the Great Animal. At the birth of the river is the head. Crater Lake. And the neck. Boundary Springs. Gwent'agabok'danda. The Nape of the Earth, its Neck. Here is the beginning, upriver to the east, toward the new light of the rising sun.

At the source of the river there are colors as bright as creation—yellow monkey flowers, green moss hugging logs that span the water, red and brown rocks coloring the bottom of the river, swarms of blue-green dragonflies that make the blue sky flow.

For thousands of years we have told stories of the river that rushes underground from the bottom of Crater Lake, then floods into a powerful river that is a source of food as well as a symbol of birth and life and death.

The river first gurgles then is born in a gush, rushing down the Cascades as fast as a child's growth. Out of control through the Rogue River Gorge, the rapids roar and scream our stories.

The river rushes past the rock home of the creator, Hapkemnas. Children Maker. He has lived here since he breathed life into the Great Animal. He lives in a cave—sharing his home with his oldest friends, the Rock People—and he watches the river rush past, day after day, season after season, century after century.

The river flows through its middle life, sometimes fast, sometimes slow, to the villages of the Human People and the Old Time homes of the Daldal brothers, the two dragonflies. In the center of the world are the Ribs of the Animal. Dat'gayawada. Here the river pauses and the deep pools speak our stories.

The river widens and slows through old age toward its death at Dit'agay'yuk!umada. Gold Beach. The Rear End of the Earth, its Tail. Near the Land of the Dead the river is swallowed by the sea, downriver to the west, toward the dying light of the setting sun.

Yet the river stretches a memory through the crash of waves, to the Village Beyond the Sunset where new beginnings are born. Far out on the sea, the river continues to tell our oldest stories.

Clouds form over the Pacific, drifting across the Cascades, bringing rain that feeds the springs that feed the river that keeps the stories going.

Here in the center of the world, along the Ribs of the Animal, I speak the ancient words and remember the beginning.

Wili yowo. Gelam. There is a house along the Rogue River.

As Mother Landscape's voice fades into the sound of the flowing river, I remove the mask of the Great Animal and summer sunshine fills the valley. This is the time to leave the winter villages, to wander to the best berry-picking places, the good hunting and fishing places, the food-gathering meadows, to the rocks where stories still live, renewing friendships and meeting relatives along the way. I saunter the long route home, exploring the Great Animal, looking for stories in the long light of the summer day and into the evening.

With Coyote's bag of masks, I'll return to the river in the fall.

The Daldal mask is two masks, one over the other. The top mask is in the shape of a dragonfly with a set of large eyeholes. Underneath is a second mask with two faces, each half-human and half-dragonfly, with two sets of eyeholes and two mouths, all overlapping. Both masks are blue-green, reminiscent of the river.

Fall is a time for coming home. In the old days the people return to their houses along the river for a time of feasting and dancing and preparation for winter. Fall is also a time for transformation.

In the Takelma mythology, the Daldal brothers journey up the Rogue River in the fall to prepare the world for the coming of the Human People.

In the spirit of the season, I return to the Ribs of the Animal on a fall day when leaves twirl off the oak trees and make rafts as they float down the river, and Indian plums are plump and ripe.

I take the Daldal mask out of the bag and put it on. I look at the river and see pieces of bodies floating past. At first I am startled. I lean over the water. Arms and legs and bobbing heads look real but not quite of this world. I turn away and hear the crash of ocean waves downriver. I know this story. I climb on top of a rock on the riverbank, gaze westward and wait for the story to come to me.

Wili yowo. There was a house at the place the Rogue River flowed wide and quiet, then mixed with the ocean at the river's mouth where waves crashed over sand bars, and in that house lived Daldal, the Giant Dragonfly with big blue wings and two heads.

Daldal stood on a hill that overlooked the river, and he saw bodies all cut through floating down the river, people with limbs all lopped off.

He said to himself, "Where do they come from? What is the matter?" For a long time people floated down the river with their legs cut right through.

Daldal packed his things and started walking upriver to find out who was killing people. A little ways up the trail he spotted a lark. He pulled out his bow, fitted an arrow, and shot. The arrow whizzed up and up and up, went through the lark's nose, piercing his nose through the middle. This was the first piercing.

The lark said, "Thank you, nephew, I am glad you made this fine hole in my nose. But you'd better watch that arrow!"

The arrow whizzed down and down and down, came straight down—THUNK!—between Daldal's two heads, went all the way through his body, and split him in half.

Now there were two of them, Elder Daldal and Younger Daldal, the dragonfly brothers. And they both went upriver looking for who was cutting up people.

I remove the outer mask, but I'm unsure which set of eyeholes to look through. Each gives me a different view of the river, and the sounds are different. I juggle the mask and find a spot where the two views come together. I gaze downriver and pick up the story.

While they walked, Younger Daldal talked all the time. His feet went clunk! on this rock, clack! on that rock, and the only time you couldn't hear him half a forest away was when they passed a thundering rapids.

Elder Daldal was quiet. He hardly said a word, and as they passed the slow, wide places in the river, his footsteps were as quiet as the flowing.

On their way they wrestled with all kinds of beings, each in his own way. They wrestled oaks bearing white acorns, oaks bearing black acorns, firs and pines and bushes and rocks. They wrestled all sorts of beings to make them strong.

Younger Daldal jumped full-body onto a tree, and with a great lot of grunting and shouting, he pulled the tree, roots and all, from the ground and tossed it into the river. "Hey, Big-nosed Daldal! Let's see you top that!"

Elder Daldal looked amused. He walked up to a tree and with sudden, intense eyes held the tree so tight in his stare, the tree finally said, "Enough!"

In this way they traveled upriver.

They arrived at a house. Inside, in the voice of an old woman, someone was saying, "Warrrm your back! Warrrm your back! Warrrm your back!"

Younger Daldal said, "Big-nosed Daldal, put on style. Stay out here in the cold if you want, I'm going inside."

He leaped onto the roof of the house, jumped down the smoke hole, and there was the old woman with her back to the fire. "Warrrm your back."

Younger Daldal lay down by the fire. The old woman leaped up and rolled him toward the flames. Then she sat on him. It was in this way she liked to kill people.

Younger Daldal couldn't move at all. He called out, "Oh, elder brother! I have blistered my back!"

Elder Daldal went inside and kicked her off his brother. Then he said in a quiet voice, "Do you think you will be a woman? People will call you camas. You will grow in the meadows. You will not be a human being. You will be food."

Nowadays she can be seen blooming in the meadows along the river. She has become good food for the people.

Elder Daldal and Younger Daldal traveled on up the Rogue River, sometimes walking alongside the crashing rapids, sometimes along the deep pools where the river flows slowly. Younger Daldal pulled trees out of the ground, and Elder Daldal stared hard. Each did his own kind of wrestling to keep him strong.

Now they heard: tut tut tut tut tut.

"Well, Big-nosed Daldal, put on style. I'm going to go see what makes that noise."

Younger Daldal walked toward the sound until he saw a house. He jumped up on top and looked down the smoke hole. He saw two old women without eyes, blind, facing each other and pounding acorns: tut tut tut tut tut.

Younger Daldal reached down and stole their food from on top of their house.

One of the women said, "Well, sister, did you eat it all up?" She said that to the other woman, who said, "How so? Perhaps it was you who ate it all up."

Younger Daldal reached down and tied their long hair together.

Now they started quarreling. One felt the other's hair pull and said, "Now she is fighting me." The other said the same thing, and they took hold of each other's hair, jumped at each other, and banged their heads: TUT TUT TUT TUT TUT!

Younger Daldal started laughing, rolling around on the roof of the house until he nearly rolled off. "Big-nosed Daldal, put on style. This is funny!" The two old women stopped. "So it's him!"

They grabbed sharp sticks and poked at him through the smoke hole. Then they jumped up on the roof and were about to poke out his eyes when Younger Daldal screamed, "Oh, elder brother!"

Elder Daldal climbed onto the roof and said, "So my grandmothers are without eyes." He took the sharp sticks from them and went inside. Younger Daldal took off stumbling toward the trail.

Elder Daldal put the points of the sticks into the fire until they were red hot. Then he crawled back on the roof and carefully put the sharp sticks into each of their eye sockets: Fssst! Fssst! Fssst! Fssst!

"Now I have made you eyes," said Elder Daldal. "Now look around you. See the trees and the river. Now you can see the world."

Elder Daldal left the two old women and continued up the trail.

He caught up with his younger brother, and the two of them traveled upriver together, now alongside the rapids, now past those pools that flowed slowly.

They came to many houses where people had been killed. Sometimes Elder Daldal helped people out of trouble. Those who were causing the problems he turned into salmon spear shafts, morning and evening stars, echoes that moved up and down the canyons, deer sinew to tie arrows with—all things to help the people.

Each place they went, Younger Daldal said, "Big-nosed Daldal, put on style." Then he walked into trouble and a few minutes later he called out, "Oh, elder brother! Come and help me!"

In this way they traveled upriver, changing things.

They came across Coyote at the falls called Ti'lomikh. Coyote had snatched up a fishing net and was thinking, "I shall catch salmon in the river."

Coyote tossed the net into the river and pulled it out, but the net was full of mice. He tossed the net back in and drew it out, but rabbits were all he caught! Again, he tossed the net. "Gophers?!"

Younger Daldal was laughing so hard the ground was shaking.

"Say, Coyote," said Elder Daldal, "it is not your place to catch salmon. People will net and spear salmon. They will catch salmon here at the falls where the river runs fast. And here they will honor the Salmon People with stories and songs and a feast. And you, Coyote, you shall eat mice and rabbits and gophers as long as the world goes on."

Coyote went on his way, poking his nose into holes, looking for someone to eat, thinking that someday he was going to change all that.

Farther upriver, Younger Daldal stopped and Elder Daldal walked on ahead. When he got to his place, he whistled like a lark, and the two brothers became flat-topped mountains along the Rogue River.

Younger Daldal is called Lower Table Rock, the one downriver towards the crashing ocean. And Elder Daldal is called Upper Table Rock, the one toward the beginning of the river, where it gurgles out of the ground.

Nowadays, in the twilight of a fall evening, anyone walking the trail from the river up the slope of either Table Rock might walk through buzzing swarms of giant dragonflies, so many that the air turns blue and loud. But up on top, the world is quiet.

From my rock on the river, I watch the myth arrive and surround me. I remove the Daldal mask and stand up. I find myself on top of an immense mesa-like rock.

I walk toward the edge across jumbled flows of basalt, past vernal pools swirling with new life, through rabbitbrush and groves of oaks and pines. The edge is an abrupt drop-off hundreds of feet to the valley floor. I look downriver and see another rock in the distance, similar to the one I am on.

"The Dragonfly brothers are here," I whisper. "More people will soon arrive."

The Gwisgwashan mask is the face of a woman, an elder of her village. She is the Keeper of Stories. Seen in the shifting light and shadows of a fire, the mask shows many expressions and moods. The face is mostly human but seems to resemble different animals at times, often changing from story to story. She has long eyelashes, and the shape of her mouth reveals a sense of wonder. There are lines of wisdom and humor around the eyeholes. One who looks through them can see beyond the circle of firelight and into the deep shadows of the forest.

Winter is the traditional storytelling season of the Takelmas. In twilight, I walk partway up the slope of Lower Table Rock to one of the old village sites. I build a small fire and take the Gwisgwashan mask out of its bag. As I put it on, the flames of the fire flicker faster and yet the fire doesn't burn down. Shadows whirl a circle dance around me. Many voices come out of one voice and join the dance, stringing together spontaneous mythic monologues that take but a moment to share yet took thousands of years to evolve.

The voices erupt at once. "I'm the best tree hacker there is!" shouts Jackrabbit. Medicine Fawn sings her medicine song, "Who creeps there about the shadows?" "I can get close to him," whispers Mudcat Woman. "All of you just floated up, but I can get close to him." Wildcat weeps for the death of his brother Panther, Grizzly Bear Woman for the loss of her children, Roasting Dead People for the death of his son. "Hey!" pleads Coyote. "Is there anyone out there? I'm stuck inside this tree!" Almost lost in the sound of the falls is the voice of an old woman: "We are Takelma, the people of the river. The salmon are our relations."

The voices end so suddenly that they echo as a single sound through the depths of the woods before fading away completely.

I remove the Gwisgwashan mask. The fire burns to coals. Darkness and silence move into the village. The first snow of the season drifts up from the valley and buries what remains of the village until there is no sign that anyone was ever here.

In the spring, I return to the Ribs of the Animal. I climb Lower Table Rock, cross the top, and sit on the southern edge above the river. I have the bag of masks with me.

Like giant dragonflies out of the blue, two helicopter sky cranes whir close to the rock on a test flight from a nearby factory. Far below, a huge machine stretches its mechanical arm and scoops sand and gravel from the heart of the river.

Are these the current culture bringers reshaping the landscape to make the world ready for the arrival of a new kind people? Are these technological trickster antics the source material for a new generation of stories?

I search through the bag for another mask to alter this intruding view of my native landscape. But all the masks have been used. I'm left with my own perspective.

I stand up and squint and the landscape shifts a little. "A clue," I whisper to myself. I take a few steps. "What's in front of me is not necessarily what I see."

As I walk, I think through the stories and the landscape shifts again. I imagine sitting on the back of a giant dragonfly, flying along the river that is the lifeblood of the world. I stretch my arms like wings and run across the rock. Again, the landscape shifts.

The words come back to me: "The beginning is a long time ago that is now." Each story leaves an impression, and Mother Landscape has a long memory. Looking through the eyeholes of the stories, I mentally shapeshift through the varied landscapes that have called the Ribs of the Animal their home.

I gaze to where the spotted magical dogs live. Coyote trots across the dry lakebed toward me. A modern magical dog? Coyote would surely think so.

"Well, what have we here?" asks Coyote. "Now that you're unmasked, what does Mister Storyteller see? The Ribs of the Animal perhaps? These are old bones for a magical pooch to gnaw on."

A springtime breeze rises from the river and dances across the top of the rock. Coyote mimes removing an imaginary mask from my face. He puts it on himself.

"Now I'm Doty the storyteller. Let's have a look … Wow, you worders are somewhat delusional, aren't you?"

"You're a silly dog. Let's go home."

"To your manuscripts?"

"No, my friend, let's sit outside on the porch. If we hurry, we can catch the last colors of the sunset over the Table Rocks."

"That's a story worth sharing. Shall we get out the masks?"

"Sometimes the masks are useful, but not this time. We don't need props to watch the sunset."

"That was profound. I think you're catching on."

"Possibly."

"Now if you could just find a practical use for your pudgy manuscripts. Fire-starters perhaps? Or fresh lining for the floor of my dog house?"

"Let's get going, my canine friend. We don't want to miss daytime shapeshift into evening."

"How poetic. Now who's being funny?"

"Right. Ready?"

"I'm always ready."

"Right again."

REMEMBERING BEAR

ACCORDING TO THE OLD ONES, THE BIG Dipper controls the seasons. We call that constellation Great Bear in the Sky. Brilliant in the night, he lumbers to his left around the North Star, the fire in his winter lodge. We stamp our circle dances in the same direction to keep the seasons in their proper order and to honor the Great Bear. Thousands of years ago, we carved symbols into rock: the foot of a human and the foot of a bear, each on one side of a counter-clockwise spiral. The message reads: Stamping dances to our left keeps Bear dancing the same way.

Able to walk upright in near-human shape, bears are our relations. In my family tradition, bears are not hunted. To kill a bear is to murder your relative. To gaze into their native-brown eyes is to gaze into human eyes.

When I was young, a black bear wandered down the mountains, through the suburbs, and ended up at my school. It was spring, and the day was as warm as summer. During the canceled recess, I pressed my nose to the classroom window and watched the bear. He was smaller than I expected. He loped across the playground, sniffing the merry-go-round, batting a swing with his paw, gazing now and again to the window and locking his playful eyes with mine. Then he crossed the street and disappeared behind a house where police cornered him and shot him dead. I cried when I heard the shots. He had been so small, hardly a cub, no farther along in his life than I was in mine. His eyes were the eyes of a child. That night a haze spread over the sky. The night turned as cold as winter. By morning it was snowing. Great Bear in the Sky had gone back to sleep.

Not so many years ago, on the last night of winter, my friends and I climbed Lower Table Rock. Stars circled overhead, bright as creation. Great Bear in the Sky had slept the winter. His snoring was the roar of the winter storms, his cool breath of hibernation the winter winds. He had chomped the moon to crescent shape, waking every false spring to snack on the moon and send it through its phases. As we passed the bear-shaped rock at the top of the trail, I patted his nose and whispered, "Wake up, Mister Bear. Springtime is coming. It's the real one this time." As it had been done in ancient times, we lit fires on the flat top of the rock to warm the earth. And we danced slow, lumbering dances, circling counter-clockwise with the nighttime dance of the stars. An old man told the myth of how the world began with a springtime creation when Children Maker made the people. The sun climbed over the eastern hills. Great Bear in the Sky woke up. His breath was the warm breath of spring.

In these seemingly un-native times, Great Bear in the Sky has dimmed in the bright lights of our cities. Earthbound bears have left their valley homes to dwell in the mountains where Great Bear in the Sky still blazes, and where the seasons still circle with the intensity of wintertime death and springtime creation.

Caves are the Old Times homes of bears. Our rock writing symbol for cave is a circle within a circle, meaning hollow, empty, all gone away.

THE BOY WHO
LIVED WITH A BEAR

On long winter nights, the people tell this story.

A long time ago on a fall day, Boy-Almost-a-Man went fishing for salmon with his five brothers. They followed the river upstream into the mountains, stopping at each of the good fishing places. In the autumn twilight, they started to pack up their catch to return home. Boy-Almost-a-Man walked on beyond the curve in the trail he had been told never to pass. His brothers called him to come back, but he kept on. There was something ahead he needed to see.

Boy-Almost-a-Man was drawn into the beauty of the long shadows of evening. He gazed at the last reddish glow of the sunset and the first pale glimmer of the rising moon. The trail crossed a mountain meadow. Near the edge of the forest, he saw the figure of a young woman picking huckleberries. She was as beautiful as the night. Her black hair and dark eyes shone in the moonlight. He slowed his pace to match hers. As she stepped out of the meadow and into the shadows of the trees, Boy-Almost-a-Man followed.

The woman walked deeper into the woods. Days and nights passed as if they were brief descriptions in a story. The first snow of the new season dusted the mountains. The woman disappeared into a hole near the base of a large tree, and Boy-Almost-a-Man followed. The way was dark and damp and smelled of recently dug earth. Boy-Almost-a-Man crawled deeper in, wriggling past tree roots and into a larger room, empty except for a bed of fir boughs. Tired from his journey, Boy-Almost-a-Man curled up on the boughs and fell asleep. Wild days and nights passed filled with snippets of stormy dreams. When Boy-Almost-a-Man awoke, his mind seemed different. He felt grown up. His name didn't fit him anymore. He listened and heard the spring songs of birds in the forest outside, and somewhere down the burrow, he heard snorting and squealing. He squinted and saw two bear cubs playing, one tumbling over the other. He turned over and saw the shape of a large she-bear sleeping beside him. He tried to think this through, but nothing made sense except the urge to go outside and find something to eat. "I will call myself No-Longer-a-Boy," he whispered. The she-bear and the cubs followed him out of their den and into the bright sunlight of a spring morning.

On the first sunny day of spring, his five brothers left the village and went hunting. They moved silently through the forest looking for signs of deer, bear, or elk. In the distance, one of the brothers saw movement. He signaled the others. They crouched, their arrows flew, and a large she-bear fell to the ground. No-Longer-a-Boy grabbed the cubs and hid in the woods. They watched in silence as the brothers approached the dead bear.

The five brothers skinned the bear and packed the hide and carcass to the village. No-Longer-a-Boy followed them home, carrying the cubs in his arms. In the village, through the spring and into the summer, No-Longer-a-Boy tried to fit in, but he was mocked by his brothers. "You're not a real man! You lived with a bear! Look how those bear cubs follow you around. Are you their father!?" When people from the village went hunting or fishing or gathering food, No-Longer-a-Boy was left behind. One night he covered himself with the skin of the she-bear, crept silently into the lodge where his brothers were sleeping, and killed them.

No-Longer-a-Boy and the bear cubs walked into the mountains to the meadow where huckleberries were ripening. They spent their days stuffing themselves, and the cubs grew and grew. As autumn shambled into winter, they journeyed deep into the woods and dug a new den. Snug inside, they slept and dreamed as mountain snow covered their tracks and filled the woods. In the village, people sat around fires in the winter dance lodge. This story was told again and again. In the spring, when the men went hunting, no one thought of killing a bear.

NATIVE WOMAN

Native Woman is on a journey. Mile by mile she is discovering herself and her culture as she walks along the Rogue River and eventually over the mountains and east to the Woman's Cave, where she will receive her true native name. Here's a piece of her story.

Near dusk, she walks the craggy trail through the Avenue of Giant Boulders. She yearns to take it all in. She glances into the darkness of caves and overhangs, side to side into each nook and cranny, her eyes following branching paths to their dead ends. Though each possibility tempts her to stray from her way, she is determined to find the river. Another step and another, carefully fitting her feet between rocks, careful not to stumble. The air cools and swirls around her as darkness settles in.

She walks onto the riverbank at moonrise. Riffles glow white. She slides into the water and surrenders to the sureness of the current. The river cradles her, makes her light. She dips her head and opens her eyes. In underwater moonlight she sees stones worn to smooth perfection. She floats through patterns that feel like childhood. She dives. She scoops up a favorite stone. She surfaces. In the water she is inside her skin, riding the river's lifeblood, flowing without effort to the deep pools downriver.

She walks the trail from the river to Diamond Lake. In autumn twilight, leaves swirl through these woods and fall to the ground. She closes her eyes and sees Earth Woman drop her blouse, slip out of her skirt, let it fall to the forest floor, and slowly recline toward her bed, where her wintertime lover waits.

Fall is a lonely season, and this walk through the autumn woods reminds her that she is alone. She notices the river is sluggish after a dry summer. Riverbanks are strewn with dead leaves. She walks past stagnant pools in the rocks where the river flowed last spring. When she steps out of her thoughts, she is standing on the shore of Diamond Lake. It is nearly dark, and her loneliness settles into a quiet grief.

The Old Ones tell a story of this place. They say that an old man discovered that his daughter had grown to love the son of his enemy. The old man was horrified. In despair, and to prevent their marriage, he transformed the young lovers into mountains, Bailey and Thielson. Diamond Lake, which lies between them, is a pool of their tears.

This evening weighs heavy and sad. She's had enough. She plunges in.

She is Earth Woman gone for a swim. She has tossed her clothes and plunged into the pool of her grief. In the cool water, naked of excess, and with the warmth of the day headed west, her skin grows tight over her bones, and she feels there is no room for anything inside her but herself.

She swims out into the lake and floats. Darkness settles onto the Cascades. Stars twinkle on until the sky looks full.

Floating on her back, she watches the harvest moon rise over the thrust of basalt that is Thielson. She watches the red and orange moonrise ... beautiful. She gathers her feelings until she is full, then sends them into the night. With fewer stars in the moonlight, there is room for what she no longer wants. She feels lighter. It is easy to float.

Moonlight surrounds Thielson, and from where she floats, it looks as though the mountain himself slips fingers of light across the lake, caressing the curvy slopes of Bailey. His touch is light and gentle, and she responds. A warm breeze brushes down Bailey's slopes and makes ripples in the lake. A breath held, and let go. She raises her head and watches the landscape of her body rise and fall in the ripples, rising out of grief and settling into the warm embrace of moonlight. She floats for longer than she remembers, and swims back to shore.

Bundling her blouse and skirt under her arm, she walks lightly into the night.

ALL NIGHT SALMON
LEAP THE FALLS

Evening Star kindles himself in the sky and sends his reflection to the surface of the river. On the eve of the spring salmon run, he flares in the purple twilight. He glances toward the growing light on the eastern horizon, anticipating the rising of the full moon. For centuries beyond remembering, native Takelmas have called this moon, When the Salmon Have Sore Backs. Evening Star listens to the drumming of the falls swelled with snowmelt and the barking of geese as they glide in and settle for the night. The moon clears the ridge and sends light flooding up and down the river, calling the sore-backed salmon home.

Evening Star gazes onto that place near the falls where the ancient village of Ti'lomikh once thrived. He sees thousand-year-old shadows of native people walking from plank house to house, preparing for the Sacred Salmon Ceremony—a net tossed in the rapids, the glint of a spear, the drying racks laid out—and around the glimmer of many fires, the sharing of stories and songs that celebrate the arrival of the Salmon People.

The moon travels the sky. The first salmon of the run strains his battered sides against the force of the falls. In sheltered nooks and crannies, the geese drift toward dreams.

Evening Star blazes in the sky and on the water. He listens to age-old whispers that linger in the shadows and to the unceasing pounding of the falls. Under his watchful eye, nighttime floats downriver as salmon strain against the current.

◇◇◇◇◇

Someone once told me that in an old house in the woods, a half mile from the Rogue River, there is a box of manuscripts by a river poet called Lampman. On a night in mid-June, Coyote and I go have a look.

The old wood-and-brick house looks abandoned, bathed in what bit of moonlight finds its path through overlapping branches of oaks and madrones. At the suggestion of Coyote, the place looks haunted. As Coyote and I approach the house, we see the yellow light of an oil lamp burning in the attic window.

Coyote glowers at the light and says, "This place starts all my dogs barking."

"It's about time," I say. "Not all of them have been awake at once for quite a spell."

"Just the same, this place wakes up my fleas and makes my fur crawl."

"Easy, boy, nothing here to fear."

"Are you crazy? We are going into an abandoned house on a full-moon night in search of some poet's old scribbling, and already there's a light in the attic as if we are expected. I'll take an old graveyard over this spooky house in these dark woods any night. At least we'd be in the open."

"Ah, yes, the power of a century of stories about this place. You think you see everything, don't you? Well, don't let those doggy eyes of yours see more than is there. Perk up your ears. Sniff the air. See for yourself. The light looks friendly. And aren't you curious, you of all dogs?"

I push on the front door and it creaks open.

"Classic. We might as well be in some horror film. Been nice knowing you, Mister Storyteller."

Once inside, Coyote expects to see dust and cobwebs, peeling wallpaper, rotting floorboards, a scuttling of critters from spiders to snooty mice to who-knows-what disgusting, coyote-gnawing, bloated bugs, and eyes—huge eyes—glowing out of the shadows … any scrap of haunted-house lore Coyote's uneasy imagination might conjure up. But what he sees inside fails to match the spirit of what he saw outside. The rooms are clean and tidy. No cobwebs. No dust anywhere, not even on the furniture. And it appears that Coyote is the only critter in the house.

We draw deep breaths as we make our way up the stairs toward the attic. We pass an open window, and night sounds drift in: the dry-leaf crackle of deer walking through the woods, the hoot of a barn owl from out back, the distant whoosh of the falls.

We walk into a flood of light in the attic. The roof is low, and there are boxes stacked along the walls. Near the window is a wood table with two chairs. An oil lamp burns in the center of the table, and near the lamp is a small box without a top. Inside is a stack of handwritten manuscripts.

"Whoa," says Coyote, glancing through the room with a worried look. "This is too weird. What a set-up!"

"Perfect," I say. "An attic that lives up to its best reputation."

"Which is?"

"A model of the world. Just listen and look around. Everything is here. There are sounds from outside … the river, animals in the woods. And here's this room that looks like any cozy shelter from any corner of the world in any century, with moonlight coming through the window. In the shadows are boxes packed with the debris of humanity. Might as well be a trash midden at the edge of some ancient village site. And look here, a hearth in the form of a lamp—warmth and light to keep at bay what looms beyond what we can see and understand. And here's a poet's table, a place to create stories of who we are and what we've done and seen, and a stack of manuscripts to give us a glimpse into a time we have almost forgotten. Pay attention, Pooch. This is not some spook playing a trick. This room might be a cave with a fire blazing and ancient writings painted on the walls. It's an invitation. Let's have a look at these papers, eh?"

Coyote and I sit in the chairs. I pick up a page yellowed at the edges and read out loud.

"A river at night whispers her secrets, and her words sound like dreams. Riverbank and meadow listen in silence. The half-moon comes closer."

Coyote and I gaze at each other. We nod without a word, as if we had discovered a voice as familiar as our own and friendly words about a place we know well. I continue.

"Upriver are the faint voices of waterfowl and the mournful cry of some bird no one knows the name of. Then there is silence, and the river flows on."

I pause and look at Coyote. We are both aware that there is a second voice in the room, speaking softly, matching word for word what I am reading. A bit hesitantly, I read a few more words, and the second voice grows louder.

"Nothing is so good as listening to the river at night. Not anything."

Coyote and I turn in our chairs and look toward the sound of the voice. Beside a stack of boxes, barely visible in the interplay of shadows and moonlight and flickering lamplight, an old man stands with his hands in his pockets, smiling. He wears a white shirt with suspenders, dark wool trousers with cuffs, and a long, black overcoat. His eyes are friendly and shine in the faint light.

We watch the man, amazed, unable to speak. The man smiles and says, "You read well. You seem to know the words as though they were your own." He stops and looks toward the window. Everyone listens. The sound of drumming drifts into the attic.

"The salmon are coming," says the man. "Let's go have a look." He glances at Coyote. "You do like salmon, don't you?"

Coyote nods. Not knowing what else to do and sensing no danger, we follow the man toward the attic door.

As we leave the room, Coyote asks, "Who are you? What's your name?"

The man looks back toward the lamp as we start down the stairs. "Lampman," he says. "Just Lampman."

As we step out the back door and into the woods, Lampman says to Coyote, "I once had a dog, and he was as fine as any man I ever knew."

Lampman leads the way into the shadows of the woods, toward the river, Coyote trotting at his heels. I bring up the rear.

◇◇◇◇◇

No light comes through these woods. Utter darkness brings a timelessness of all nights made into one, and this night might be any night in the history of forests. Not even the light of the full moon finds its way past the canopy of trees. I am thinking that were Lampman not with us, I would never find even a trace of this woodland path. I follow Lampman and Coyote not by sight, but by sound, and our walking is not the only sound. Despite the darkness, the forest breathes life. The overhead maze of twisted branches is a sanctuary for birds. As the three of us walk through the woods, the songs and calls and stirrings of night birds float out of the trees. They mix with the cool air and swirl around them like a gentle breeze, or air moved by the soft-feathered wings of birds, or the breathing of ancient trees. Each step is a step out of time and into the depths of nighttime as it has always been.

As we approach the edge of the woods we see a glimmer of moonlight and an orange glow from the fires at the village of Ti'lomikh. We walk out of the trees and into a meadow. The sounds of the village are distinct. We hear the singing of each word of each song, each drumbeat, the foot-stamping of dancing, choruses of conversation. The night pounds with the electric pulse of a village celebrating the arrival of the salmon.

Lampman breaks the silence of their voices. He turns and asks me, "Have you heard stories of the Salmon Ceremony?"

"Sure," I say.

"And being a storyteller, you are aware of the power of stories to take us beyond what we might imagine?"

"And more," I say.

"Good," says Lampman. "Then let's walk into this story. If we pay attention, we'll be different people by the time this story ends."

"Talk, talk, talk," says Coyote. "Are we there yet? When do we get to the salmon?"

"Patience, my hungry friend," I say. "We've got all night, and more."

Coyote bounds toward the river and I follow. Lampman pauses at the edge of the meadow, looks back to the trees, and speaks softly to himself.

"Do you remember hearing the grouse? In the dark forest she sounds like the beating of a great heart, or, in the desert, an old man sitting in the moonlight beating an ancient drum. Do you remember?"

Lampman crosses the meadow and joins us. We climb down the steep bank to the river and enter the Old Time village of Ti'lomikh.

The village is swelled with people, those who live here as well as visitors from other villages: Daldani, Gwenpunk, Didalam, Hagwal, Gelyalk.

At one of many fires, an old woman of the village speaks to a gathering of travelers who have just arrived. She wears a traditional basket cap and buckskin dress decorated with beads and dentalium shells. A shawl covered with drawings of dragonflies is draped over her shoulders. She leans on a carved wooden cane. Her speech is a mixture of formal Takelma, Chinook Jargon, and native sign language flowing together in a way that makes clear the meaning and poetry of her message. Her speech is ancient and stylized. Only elders know how to do this well.

Coyote and Lampman and I join the others and listen.

"This river is Gelam, and we are Takelma, the people of the river. The salmon are our relations. Each year the Salmon People come to our village during this moon when their backs are strained. Like you, they have traveled along rivers and creeks. And like people everywhere, they have suffered. By the time the salmon reach this middle stretch of the river, they look battered. Their fins are torn and their sides bruised. They've struggled against miles of strong rapids and leaped many a waterfall on their journeys upriver. By the time the salmon reach our village of Ti'lomikh, their backs are sore, at the very least. This is a triumph and a time of celebration.

"As they pass our home, we pray and we sing for the salmon, we dance for the salmon, and we tell stories of the Salmon People. We also fish for the salmon. But in taking, we give back. The first salmon who offers himself to the net is caught and gutted and put on a drying rack. For as long as it takes for that salmon to dry, no more salmon are taken from the river. Thousands leap the falls and continue their journey to the beginning of their world. Like us and all our relations, they want to live a long time. To the sounds of flutes, divers return the bones of that first salmon to the bottom of the river. As soon as he has dried, the fishing starts again. And that night, we feast."

Coyote and Lampman and I walk into the heart of the village. All night the drums beat, feet stamp, voices sing the old songs in honor of the Salmon People. Evening Star blazes bright in the sky. The moon travels overhead. The drumming of the falls fills the air. And all night salmon leap the falls, dancing their dance of survival.

We walk past several plank houses. Singing and firelight spill out and flood the night. We walk past outdoor fires where more people gather. Some play guessing games, tossing gambling bones and singing. Some spin stories. Others gossip and talk with folks they haven't seen for a spell. Coyote and Lampman and I make our way to the edge of the river and sit on the sand.

An old man sits on a stone chair. He fasted for five days to be the salmon myth teller, and now a crowd gathers to listen to his stories. The old man glances across the river to the rocks below the falls. As he watches an elderly fisherman toss a net into the river, the old man tells, with fluid gestures and a voice as full as the falls, the myth of the salmon.

"Evening Star and Morning Star were the first owners of this place. They wrestled everyone who came here and killed them. They allowed no one to fish."

The old man describes how Elder Dragonfly, one of the culture-bringing brothers, pinned the two stars to their present places in the sky and made the salmon free to all the people.

"Later on, the Dragonfly Brothers came across Coyote here at the falls. Coyote had snatched up a fishing net and was trying to catch salmon. But all he caught were mice and rabbits and gophers. "Elder Daldal sent him on his way. Then he carved a chair into the rock near the falls and a groove next to it to hold the handle of a dip net. He said to the river, 'People will feed each other here. They shall not kill one another. It will be this way as long as the world goes on.'"

The old man points to the falls and says, "Look, the first visitor has arrived!"

In the spray of the falls, the elderly fisherman pulls the first salmon from the net. He carries him to a drying rack on the rocks. Others gather around and help prepare the fish.

As the old storyteller stands up and starts to walk away from the story chair, he turns and says, "Does anyone else want to share a story?"

Coyote starts to stand up, but a glance and a gesture and a whispered "wait" from me holds him back. Several people aim encouraging nudges at their friends, but it is Lampman who finally stands up. He looks at the people, nods and smiles, and then gazes at the river. He walks to the chair, sits down, and with incredible skill, he weaves his story of the salmon.

A long time ago, an old woman told me this story.

We are all related, she said, the people of the sea, of the air, of the land. And the people who move between worlds: the Rock People, the Fire People, all our relations. There was a time when we spoke the same language. Perhaps that time is coming again. Meanwhile, our myths are as vivid as our memories of those times, and the stories—even the tragic ones—teach us to remember all of our relations and to care for them … and what can happen if we forget.

In a village along the river, near the ocean, there was a boy who was always hungry. His parents fed him little, and what he did get was the meager leavings of everyone else's meals. His mother gave him what was left of his father's catch after others had eaten their fill: the head of Dog Salmon, the tail of Water Snake, the guts of Seal. It was never enough. He left home hungry and journeyed to the mouth of the river and fell down on the sand. His belly roared with hunger. He struggled on the beach, writhing, the roar of the sea and the roar of hunger bursting his head, salt tears streaming down his face. He turned over like sea waves roared and turned over on the sand. He turned into someone new!

He swam deep in the water, downriver toward the sea. He opened his eyes wide and saw far and deep. His mouth opened as he swam through the river's mouth. He breathed water as he once breathed air. He tasted the thickening salt of the sea. His eyes widened until he couldn't close them. They felt no sting of salt as he swam into the vastness of the ocean. He clearly saw the smallest stones at the bottom of the sea. They shimmered and shone like stars.

He had moved from one world to another. He had become one of the Salmon People. He was called Salmon Boy.

Ahead, in the dim depths of the sea, he saw his new relations. Their watery voices surrounded him, whispering of food.

"The flow of the river is strong and we are tired. We have come here to rest in the rocking of the sea. We are as hungry as you are. We must eat and grow strong for our final upriver journey. Help us find the Herring People. This is our feast day!"

With a swish of their green tails they turned and swam toward the home of the Herring People. Salmon Boy swam behind them, following close, swept along in the current of their desire for food.

He saw shapes of sea-myth characters grow out of the shimmering stones: She Who Walks Backwards Going Home, the woman who was half turned to stone by the lonely howls of Wolf Whale, Seal Mother who laughs at the antics of her children, the high whistle of Giant Sea Snake who haunts the depths, Loon Woman rising out of seaweed and flying through water as if it were air. And somewhere deep down below the shimmering star-stones, He Who Changes the World began to stir from his long sleep.

Salmon Boy followed his people to that place on the horizon where the sun and moon dipped into the sea, where day forever closed into night, and they arrived at the village of the Herring People. It was a feast day indeed! The water was thick with eggs from the bottom to the surface of the sea. Salmon Boy swished through the eggs as he ate them, leaping out of the water and crying, "We are Hungry! Hungry! Hungry!"

But He Who Changes the World woke up and rattled his underwater realm. The great house posts that connected the sea to the sky shook and shifted. The moon shattered into pieces, and rain fell in a flood.

The salmon fled the village of the Herring People, swimming toward the mouth of the river, their mouths tasting the first swell of fresh water as they swam through the river's mouth and started their upriver journey toward the end for which they were born.

Salmon Boy was no longer hungry. His belly roared with fullness. He jumped as he swam, smacking his tail on the surface, screaming, "Heyo! I eat and I leap! I breathe! I am Salmon Boy!!"

He was fully himself. He breathed water. He tasted water. He felt joy in the water.

Then water turned to darkness.

As they passed the shores of his old village, he felt a spear-thrust move through him, felt it lift him out of the river, felt the shock of wind in his mouth. His wide eyes caught a glance of his own father the fisherman, spearing one more salmon for dinner.

He writhed on the riverbank, his eyes still and open. No voice of the sea came from his mouth as his father split him open and emptied his belly. No voice of the river came as his mother stretched him across the drying rack. All day he shriveled in the sun, his wide eyes staring upriver toward the beginning of the river, upriver toward the end of the salmon, upriver ...

There is a long silence as the words settle into the hearts of the listeners. Then people start to whisper, and slowly, conversation grows back to normal. Lampman gets up and walks back along the river.

Coyote says to me, "Now that's a pretty good story. But I want to hear all about Lampman's dog. There are worse critters than poets who like dogs."

Before Lampman can launch into his favorite dog story, the drumming around the fires suddenly stops. Singing stops. Talking stops. Except for the rush of the river, the village is quiet. People listen. Faint at first and then growing to fill the silence, the sound of flute music drifts across the river and into the village. The people at Ti'lomikh look to the slow-flowing water above the falls. They watch in silence as five young men leap into the icy water. Each one dives deep and places the bones of the first salmon in the gravel of the riverbed, back to the source. This sacred gesture is as ancient as the river itself, and all people born at Ti'lomikh are born with paintings of that moment already vivid in their memories.

Coyote and Lampman and I spend the night walking from fire to fire, listening to stories, dancing Old Time dances, singing songs that praise the salmon. As night grows old, each person in the village casts an inward eye to the night when the salmon feast begins, especially Coyote. He figures that he'll blend in just fine with the rest of the people and stuff himself with salmon until his doggy sides bulge.

At the edge of the village, in a quiet moment by himself, Lampman stands on the sand and speaks to the river.

"Do you remember listening to the birds just before the sun rises up? They're still a little sleepy, and they sing of the world waking up, just like creation is happening all over again. Then light comes out of nighttime, like a mystery revealed, and the world wakes up and sings praise to the creator. Do you remember?"

In the dim moments before dawn, the fires burn low. The people at Ti'lomikh gather in close circles and speak prayers to the coming sun. Morning Star kindles himself in the sky. The moon disappears over the ridge, and the purple light of sunrise grows in the east. Geese wake up and take flight in a clamor of splashing and barking and flapping of wings. Under Morning Star's watchful eye, morning floats downriver as salmon continue their struggle against the strength of the falls.

THE BOY WALKED INTO THE SUN, HIS FATHER INTO THE MOON

ALONG THE KLAMATH RIVER, THE PEOPLE TELL this story.

At Sundown Place, there was a woman pounding acorns inside her house. The fire was low, sending out small flickerings of light, and in that firelight, the woman's baby boy was playing.

Now the baby became hungry. He crawled across the floor mats, the fire lighting his eyes. He crawled into the shadows where his mother was working. He crawled up on her, making hungry sounds. But carefully, gently, she pushed him off, and she kept on pounding acorns. Again, he crawled up on her. Hunger was in his belly! But carefully, gently, lovingly, she pushed him off. And she kept on pounding acorns in the shadows of the house.

Near sundown, all was quiet. The woman stopped pounding. She looked around. She listened. No sounds.

The baby was gone!

The woman pushed open the door and ran outside. The sun was going down, the full moon rising. She ran around the house, looking in different places, but she could not find her baby anywhere.

She went back inside, sat in the shadows, and kept on pounding acorns for a long time … long time …

In the light of the full moon, her husband came home from hunting. She said, sobbing, "I—I lost the baby. He's crawled away. Our baby is gone!"

The husband threw the deer he had brought on the floor mats near the fire. He tossed his bow and his arrows into a carved box, clacking the lid down. He ran outside, frantically searching for the baby, from tree shadow to shadow, all night under the white moon.

Next morning, as the sun rose, it lit the trail of the crawling baby at that place the baby had crawled out of the house. The father started walking east, following the trail of his son. That night the moon started shrinking, rising later, started chasing the sun.

The father kept following his boy, and farther to the east he saw his son's footprints and knew that he had begun to walk. He saw the places the boy was spending the nights resting, and he saw where he played along the way.

The days were cloudless and sunny, and the late nights were full of the shrinking moon.

The father kept on, never eating, weeping as he walked, and soon he saw the place where the boy had made a bow.

On he went, day after day, night after night. He saw where his son had built a fire and places he left his father food along the trail: cooked birds and squirrels and other small animals.

He kept on, and after a time he noticed by the size of the footprints that his son had grown quite tall, and he found the place where he had killed a deer. The father ate the roasted deer meat that had been left for him, then kept traveling the trail toward the east, crying as he walked.

Now the nights were darker. Only the curved brow of the moon was showing in the sky.

Farther to the east, in the faint light, the father saw something in the trail that told him his son was only a little ahead of him. He went on down the trail, and at sunrise he heard his son singing. Woodpecker scalps, bright red in the dawn, had been left by the side of the trail. He knew he was close, the singing was loud and clear … an ancient song, a power song, a sacred song.

oo-na-ha

oo-na-oon

na-wee-ee-hee

oo-na-ha

oo-na

sun and moon

together we will fly

sun and moon sometimes

sun and moon always

oo-na-ha

oo-na-oon

na-wee-ee-hee

oo-na-ha

oo-na

The boy was thinking, "Poor man, my father. He's traveling day and night. I'll sing and let him find me."

In the dawn light, far to the east, the father caught up with his son. The boy said, "I thought you would turn back from here."

"No," his father said. "I will go with you." He was surprised to see that his son's eyebrows were bright red, the color of woodpecker scalps. And the boy was amazed at the whiteness of his father's hair.

"Go back after your hunting things," said the boy, "and then you may go with me."

The father traveled back along the trail toward his old home at Sundown Place. When he got there, it was strange. He noticed moss growing all over the outside planks of the house, and the trees all around were much larger than when he'd left. Years had gone by.

The father crouched down and crawled inside. It was dark. The fire was dead. He put his hand into the fire pit, and under a heap of ash, he felt the charred bones of his wife, who had died a long time ago. No one knows how she died. Maybe old age. The place smelled musty. The floor mats were rotting away. Years had gone by.

The father moved through the house, searched through the darkness, and found the carved box, the one with his hunting things. And then he started back along the trail, toward the east, where his son was waiting.

He got to that place at sunrise, one moon later. His son pounded incense root and bathed his father in it, and then they traveled together to Sunrise Place.

They still live there, mostly traveling the world each by himself, the father through the night, his son through the day. But sometimes they travel together, in the daytime.

The boy had walked into the sun, his eyebrows shining, and his father into the moon, his white hair wild in the night.

Forever. And ever. And ever.

MOTHER LANDSCAPE

MOTHER LANDSCAPE SPEAKS VOICES THAT ARE HEARD by those who have chosen to listen. For centuries, it has been the art of native storytellers to place themselves within earshot of those voices. Storytellers journey to places Mother Landscape is known to visit and to sacred places she calls home. In quiet moments in the depths of night, the tellers hear whispered words. They learn the words until they grow into memories that seem their own. Eventually, they share them as stories.

There are places where the voices of Mother Landscape have been heard and her stories painted and carved on cliffs and in caves. A few of these pictures show the storyteller as she abandons her role as narrator to join her story as a dramatic participant. In firelight, in the depths of a winter evening, characters come alive and speak directly to each other and to those in the audience. This is the most ancient spark of performance.

The storyteller's words sizzle with depth. Layers of truth emerge as her story swells beyond sound to include a visual canvas of gestures and movements. Like the story itself, shadows cast on walls by firelight loom larger than the event. What is real transcends itself into what is possible. Not only is the storyteller transformed, so are her listeners.

In the pictures they are often portrayed as myth characters. Perhaps those who were most deeply touched by the stories were the artists who were inspired to create the pictures. If one looks long enough at the images, it isn't hard to imagine that there is a time in each story when listeners become so engaged in the narrative that they leap up and join in a telling that soon becomes a dance drama.

When we visit the cliffs and the caves and view these pictures, we are reminded to remember.

WAITING FOR ROCK
OLD WOMAN

AT THE COVERED BRIDGE NEAR SUNNY VALLEY, Coyote and I begin our search for the ancient rock that represents Rock Old Woman, a medicine woman in Takelma myths and folklore and one who lives in the hearts of the people.

"Trust me," says Coyote.

"Right," I say.

"Really," says Coyote. "I know where she is."

"Perhaps."

"Good. It's inspiring to watch a human attempt to gaze beyond his limited vision and ponder mythic possibilities. There's still hope for your folks! Perhaps you might stretch your brain and try to understand that there is a difference between the eternal spirit of Rock Old Woman and the rock that people say look like her. If you can do that, we'll get to somewhere interesting in this story."

Coyote's smirk shifts to a scowl as he concentrates on a new thought.

"Well, it seems you're right about one thing. That rock is sacred to the human beings. That's where Rock Old Woman sat down to rest. And for a few short centuries it's been a handy place to leave offerings. But not so long ago, she stood up and went for a walk. She's still wandering around.

Stick with me, Mister Storyteller, and you'll learn something. It's time we arrived at the source."

On these rare occasions when Coyote is right, he makes a long speech about it. Every full moon or so, a crumb of doggy wisdom pounces out of the depths of Coyote's narcissistic brain and makes sense to me. Mostly in agreement, and up for an adventure, we drive toward Sunny Valley, identified by Coyote as "the source." As we journey through the mountain landscape, my memory time-travels. To feel inside the story, I speak the words out loud. Coyote pretends to be napping.

For years I search for the medicine rock called Rock Old Woman. I walk traces of Old Time Indian trails, down gullies, through shady woods of ferns and creeks, along the ruts of wagon roads, down the car-body-littered roadbeds of Pacific Highway and Route 99, and along the graveled shoulder of Interstate 5. I search for the clearing, the exact place where she stood. For years I see her ghost in every flat-topped, mossy rock along the way. I carry with me old maps, scraps of stories scribbled in field notes, and bits of narratives that survive from native oral literature. But maps and stories and intuition bring me back to the gash in the mountain called Sexton Summit and the rumble and diesel stink of long-haul trucks crawling through the pass.

Standing on what's left of the old highway above the pass, my mind fills in the landscape that was blasted away to improve the road. I see a grassy valley, the old Indian trail crossing the summit, Rock Old Woman covered with offerings of salmon and camas and Indian plums. Years later there is a stage stop, a ranch house, a barn, and an orchard of apple and plum trees. With the first wagons, the last native people to walk the trail pause at the summit and thank Rock Old Woman for their good health as their ancestors have done for centuries. They leave their gifts of food and whisper her name. Those who know Rock Old Woman well call her Grandmother. They sit in silence and listen to her song. They hear other words in the breeze that journeys gently through the pass, rustling the leaves of madrones and oaks. In the distant village called Daldanik, away from the medicine rock in a rocky place along the creek, someone is telling her story.

"According to the Old Ones, when the world was first made by Hapkemnas the Children Maker, Rock Old Woman was given the power to get rid of medicine people who were twisted in their ways and caused sickness and death. She was given a stone pipe, a rock bucket, several other stone tools, and most importantly, a song.

"As she sang her song and her victim smoked the pipe of death, Rock Old Woman heated stones and dropped them into the bucket, boiling the person's heart, stirring it with a paddle until the one who caused sickness and death in others had died. Sexton Mountain tied his hair into a topknot like he was going to war. He dusted his forehead with white paint. He wrenched loose the medicine person's arm and danced with it, singing his medicine song from the red of sunset to the orange of sunrise. To this day, Sexton Mountain's topknot is visible in the shapes of trees on the summit.

"This is how we get rid of bad medicine. Since before the myths, we have included her name in our prayers for good health. She stands in stone with her tools around her, inspiration to soon-to-be medicine people and a contemplative image to those who live long lives without sickness. Her medicine always works. As we rest at the summit, we leave her gifts. Sometimes we lean against her and draw strength for our long walk ahead. We thank her and whisper, 'Rock Old Woman … Dan Mologol … Grandmother.' From deep in our memories of the myths, she answers us with her song."

Down the slope from Sexton Summit, the old Indian trail crosses Leaf Creek near the covered bridge. Later, the Applegate Trail, Pacific Highway, and Route 99 use this same crossing. In 1846, as an emigrant wagon train camps at the crossing, sixteen-year-old Martha Leland Crowley dies of typhoid fever. Family and friends bury her nearby. Since that day, the creek is called Grave Creek. Though locals still passionately share her story, if one pauses by her grave, the story tells itself.

This ancient creek crossing is a place where stories linger after people have left. Without words, a story survives as a ghostly presence in the place where it lived. Stories find a voice in the crash of a waterfall, a fall breeze that twirls leaves into the creek, the night steps of deer browsing through a meadow. As people cross the creek, they carry their stories with them. Where they settle for a spell, their stories find a home. They mingle with the varied voices of the landscape. They mix with the lingering tales of generations of people who passed through before. They are retold by those who stop by for a visit. After the words are silent, a few of the stories remain. This crossing is such a place.

After years of searching, I begin to believe Rock Old Woman is gone from us forever. I picture her remains as a mound of gravel and debris under the truck-rutted lanes of Interstate 5. This belief vanishes one evening in October when Coyote insists that Rock Old Woman is still wandering the countryside, and, with some patience, she will find us. Coyote and I arrive at Grave Creek at sunset and sit on rocks near the crossing.

"We're done searching," says Coyote. "Now we wait, and this is the right place."

"How do you figure that?"

"You said it yourself. Everyone passes by here with stories in their satchels."

"It's getting dark."

"Perfect," says Coyote.

"Maybe we should build a fire."

"Let's keep it dark. We'll see more. And look, the moon is paying us a visit."

"Maybe you critters see more without the sun in Sunny Valley, but ..."

"Hush," says Coyote. "Someone's coming."

At first, I notice little beyond the blur of headlights and the rumble of the freeway. As my eyes adjust to the gathering darkness, I listen for sounds beyond the noise of traffic ... and the night world opens.

Each shifting shadow flickers with an inner light as it becomes a story borrowed from history and myth. Whispered words and story sounds ride the riffles of the creek. An evening breeze slips down the mountain. It mixes the sounds and makes the shadows dance, reshaping the stories as it carries them across the creek.

Coyote and I listen carefully, trying to make sense of the jumbled sounds we are hearing. Sounds invite pictures, and together they turn quickly into a tone poem of the past.

1933. A linguist in his Model T Ford drives across the covered bridge and parks. An old woman walks to the creek crossing. She stands silently, a concentrated look on her face as she digs deep into her memory to remember the Takelma name for Leaf Creek. "Takhta'asin," she whispers. "They call it Grave Creek now." Grass grows tall, covering graves in the meadow. Gold seekers drift past and take little notice.

Scrambling for precious metal shifts to grabbing for prime land. And war. Halloween, 1855. Soldiers die in the Battle of Hungry Hill … the Battle of Bloody Spring … their unmarked graves here, near Fort Leland. Twenty Indians die in the same battle, but no one knows where they are buried. Nine years earlier, native shadows dart from tree to tree on ridgetops that ring the valley, watching the first wagon train rattle through the creek. A legend floats over Martha Leland Crowley's grave: five Indians from the Indian War buried in the same grave as her. Anything is possible. Some folks don't believe it. Before that, two decades of mountain men fur trappers splash through the creek on their treks into the mountains where trapping and hunting is good. New Ones share a fire with the last of the Old Ones, who not only remember the ancient myths but still live them.

A procession of healers. Old Time medicine people cross the creek: Mudcat Woman, Acorn Woman, Medicine Fawn, Sparrow Hawk who is Yellow Between His Claws, Husu Chicken Hawk who is Red-Tailed Hawk. Medicine mountains are guardian spirits. They watch long-lived centuries pass by. Altawayakwa, who is Sexton Mountain, and his eastern brother, Altakanxita. The great canoe of beings rests on his slopes after surviving the Takelma world flood. Many mountain relations circle the Takelma world. As culture watchers, they keep an eye on things.

Native generations cross the creek to food-gathering meadows. They dig roots for making baskets on Hungry Hill. The old name is Takwelsaman, On Top of Roots. Generations cross the creek toward good fishing and hunting places. They visit relations in the villages of Ckactun, Lathpaltha, Daldanik, Titalam, on their way to the salmon ceremony at Ti'lomikh.

A procession of storytellers. Myth characters walk with them: Panther and his younger brother Wildcat, the Daldal brothers, the White Duck sisters, Coyote, Jackrabbit. A long procession molds the landscape into stories.

Five figures appear in the shadows. A native family crosses the creek. A young girl tugs on the skirt of her mother and asks, "Will we get to visit Dan Mologol tonight?" "Yes," her mother says. "She is waiting for us."

I'm on my feet and running down the trail, trying to keep up with the family. "Come on!" I yell to Coyote. "If we follow them, we'll find her!"

Coyote hesitates. He looks a little nervous about following what appear to be ghosts, but his adventurous spirit takes over. He pounces onto the trail and lays out his tail.

"I'm right behind you!"

Walking is easy along the road through town. We turn uphill, following the mostly abandoned Pacific Highway with its faded yellow line, cracked asphalt, and concrete shoulders. Here the town lights fade out of sight and the woods turn deep and dark. A stray dog slinks across the road and disappears into the trees. I get glimpses of the family ahead of us. Sometimes they walk off the road and into the forest, following a trail invisible to me. Then they appear again, walking the road as if it lay over the top of the old trail. Despite changes in the landscape, they know the way. Coyote is close behind, unusually quiet.

As we walk into the canyon, the road turns to gravel and parallels the freeway. The sudden appearance of oncoming headlights is blinding, but eventually the road turns back into the woods and the freeway is gone, save the sound of traffic. We wade a mountain creek and walk through a logging site where the road has been churned to mud and dried into deep ruts. Moonlight makes the cut-over land stark and dramatic. Back in the woods, I hear faint voices ahead of us but cannot see the family.

This short stretch of Pacific Highway is paved. Deeper into the trees, the pavement disappears under a layer of duff covered with moss. The moon hides behind ridges, and darkness fills the space where moonlight had shone. There is just enough light to follow the road. Here, for the first time, highway and old trail are indistinguishable. The forest has reclaimed this route and made it good for walking. This only lasts for a few feet. The road and woods end abruptly. There is a drop-off to the freeway many feet below. Ahead is a steep, bare slope of loose rock, criss-crossed by dangerous traces of animal trails. The only handholds across the slippery scree are a few old roots from trees that are no longer there. This way looks treacherous, chancy at best. The family is nowhere to be heard or seen.

Coyote trots up to me. "Whoa. You're no longer the leader. There's a better critter trail back a ways. You missed it. Follow me. I know the way."

Back in the woods, I hear animals scurrying through thick brush and owls hooting from tree to tree.

"They speak an ancient language," whispers Coyote. "If you stand here long enough, you'll hear the words of the dead. Let's get going!"

Walking into this woodland mixture of shifting shadows and strange night sounds feels like stumbling into Mythtime. What looks real might just as easily be the dream-like landscape of an Old Time story, remembered and shaped by generations of tellers as it travels along the moon-speckled path of oral tradition.

In the myths, supernatural beings roam these woods at night. They are half-animal, half-human. One of them lives here. He has a big light above his head. Another has the horns and body of a deer. And here I am, I'm thinking, a mad storyteller wandering these woods at night, led along trails I can barely see by some crazy light-headed, half-animal, half-human myth character. I whisper a few of his native nicknames ... Mister Coyote ... Coyote Old Man ... Grandfather.

We walk deeper into the shadows where the world of the woods looks jumbled, mixed up. The old trail splits in several directions, and moss-covered pieces of Pacific Highway are tilted on end, their jagged, broken ends draped with ferns. It looks like a scene from an end-of-the-world film. I expect to see the toppled ruins of the Statue of Liberty around the next bend. I imagine Rock Old Woman has come to a similar end. We have walked into a landscape that lives beyond geography. Here in the debris swell the seeds of a new generation of stories.

Coyote stares at the concrete-and-asphalt rubble and chuckles. "Maybe this is the future fate of the information highway."

"You're a funny pooch. Too many facts? Not enough stories about you?"

"That's right!"

"More than likely," I say, "this is what happens to the stories we forget to listen to."

"Same thing."

I follow Coyote as he pushes on through the trees. As we climb higher, the forest thins and the trail is easier to see. At the old summit, we walk into a clearing and the trail ends abruptly in a steep road cut.

Though they were ahead of us and there seems to be only one way through the woods, the Takelma family has vanished. I look around. No one. We are alone at the pass. Dozens of feet below is the roar and haste of Interstate 5. I pull a crumpled map out of my pocket. I angle it into the moonlight and turn it in my hands, trying to line up what's left of the landscape with the few lines on the map.

"See?" I say to Coyote. "We're standing on the edge of what's left of the old highway. Here's a couple of apple and plum trees from the orchard. The old pass was a gentle slope from here to just across the freeway." I point to the empty air above the pass. "The barn was there, and Rock Old Woman just behind the barn, about where those freeway lanes are."

Coyote appears distracted. He's humming some old song to himself, getting louder with each verse. He looks at the freeway and the empty space above it. He howls a long and angry howl. He leaps off the trail and into the air. When he comes down, it's as if he's landed on a mythic stage crowded with listeners. Gesturing wildly, he screams a monologue that is spontaneous and dramatic.

"Imagine Dan Mologol's final day here on the pass! The mountain called Altawayakwa moans with the creak and whine of heavy machinery. Some politician visits this place, some two-bit politician who gained votes from the building of a newfangled road. He's walking around and hobnobbing with the workers when he spots a stone pipe on the ground. He picks it up and looks it over. Someone suggests that it looks like it could still be smoked. A pipe smoker himself, the politician is intrigued. He takes tobacco out of his coat pocket, packs the pipe, and draws a puff to see if it works. And work it does! Altawayakwa yanks his arm off and dances his Old Time dance, singing like the wind, waving the severed arm and shaking his topknot under a blood-red sunset, clear to the light of dawn! Ha!!"

Coyote grabs a dead branch from under an apple tree. He swings it over his head. He yips and howls. He skips down the trail.

He freezes in his tracks.

Sounds from deep in the woods bristle his tail. Old Time singing drifts up and over the pass like an evening breeze. Words flutter past us, getting louder as they gather speed and blow down the old Indian trail.

Coyote bounds after the song. Somehow this old dog of a trail guide knows every turn and twist. I jog to keep up. In half the time it took us to get to the summit, we are back at the creek crossing. When I catch up with Coyote, he's leaning against a rock, breathing easy like he never left the place. I sit down. We wait in silence.

In this still moment before sunrise, mist settles along Grave Creek. As the sun slips over the ridge and fills Sunny Valley with autumn light, we hear an echo of the Old Time song ... the song that inspires Rock Old

Woman to take care of her people, the song she sings as she does her best healing, the song that reminds us to remember our stories. We hear her singing in the song of the rising sun, the song of the morning breeze moving across the valley, the song of many stories crossing the creek. I look up and catch a glimpse of an old woman. The singing gets louder as she wades the creek. She crosses the meadow, pauses at a grave, and disappears into the mist. The sun is fully up. Across the valley, Interstate 5 roars with morning traffic.

"See?" says Coyote.

"What?" I say.

"I told you she was here."

"Right."

"Trust me," says Coyote.

"All right," I say. "Just this once."

JOURNEY TO THE
LAND OF THE DEAD

COYOTE'S PAW IS A NATIVE VILLAGE WHERE the Klamath River flows through a deep canyon. In the village are grassy meadows, groves of oaks and pines, rock walls, cairns, a dance ring. A creek flows between the winter houses and the graveyard. An ancient trail connects Coyote's Paw to other villages both upriver and downriver. This area was continually inhabited by native people for thousands of years.

These days, Coyote's Paw is a peaceful, quiet place. When I sit in the village, I listen to what my ancestors heard: the rushing of the river, the wind in the oak trees, the screech of a red-tailed hawk. Sometimes I hear voices and laughter from people rafting through the canyon, echoes of sounds that have always been here. But mostly it is quiet. And if I listen carefully, I hear the words of stories as they were told in the community house or in the shade of Grandmother Pine. And the stories, like the people, have traveled along the river for a long time.

At Coyote's Paw, the people tell this story.

On a fall morning, a man and a woman were married in a meadow along the banks of the Klamath River. The sun rose bright red, scattering stars of light across the morning, across the surface of the sleepy river. The man and the woman were married in the dawn light.

That night, as the sun sank red downriver, the night turned cold, filled with stars. In the middle of the night, the woman got out of bed to put more wood on the fire. Walking across the dirt floor in the dim light, she stumbled and fell into the coals and was burned so badly that she died.

Her husband woke up as she screamed. He saw a flash of light and a red glow. The husband got out of bed and followed the red glow out of the house and along the river trail. The night stars were sharp and reflected in the still flow of the river. The husband followed the glow as it rose into the sky and joined the walking stars of the Milky Way, who travel quickly toward the Land of the Dead. But now it was night, and those who traveled that trail were sleeping. He could see the glow of their campfires along the edge of the Milky Way.

The husband kept on, running as fast as he could, getting nearer and nearer the glow. When he came up right behind it, he saw the shape of his wife inside a circle of red light.

Then it was daytime, and she went traveling the sky trail. Her husband followed behind, trying to keep up. Looking down, he could see the rapids in the river where it rushed through a canyon.

On he went, catching up with her at night as she camped along the trail, then nearly losing her in the daytime as she moved with the swift running of the stars.

For five days he followed his wife along the trail of the Milky Way, and finally, on the fifth night, he arrived at the Land of the Dead.

He could hear music, people singing and dancing and having a happy time. For a long while he watched from a distance, listening to the songs, watching the smiling faces of the dead, their sure feet moving to the singing and the rhythm of deer-hoof rattles. And he could see his wife, dancing among the dead ones.

He moved in closer and asked the fire-tender if he could have his wife back, but the fire-tender shook his head no. "Not now," he said.

The husband sat down. He was tired from all that running, and he fell asleep.

And the singing and the dancing went on and on, and on through the night ...

In the morning, the red sun started rising and woke him up. He looked to where the dead ones had been dancing. They were sleeping, their bodies like white ash.

The fire-tender walked up to him and gave him a stick, a fire-poker. He told the husband to gently poke each of the sleeping dead ones. When one of them rose up, that one would be his wife.

The husband started poking the white-ash bodies, one here, one there ... carefully ... gently ... He came to one that had a bit of a red glow around it. Gently he poked it, and it rose up, and when he looked closely, he saw the shape of his wife.

He picked her up, put her over his shoulder, and started back along the trail.

At first she weighed nothing at all. But as he carried her nearer his home, she grew heavier and heavier.

He put her down to rest. There was a flash of light ... and she was gone.

He followed her back along the trail, found her again at the Land of the Dead, put her over his shoulder, and carried her back toward his home. Again, she got heavier and heavier.

But he was getting close. He could feel the cool air near the river. They were nearly to the door of the house, but he was so tired and she was so heavy, he had to put her down.

Again there was a flash ... and she was gone.

Two more times he traveled to the Land of the Dead and failed to bring his wife home. The fire-tender told him he could not try again. He was told to go back home and in a short time he and his wife would be together.

It was dark when he got home. The stars were bright. He went inside his house, lit the fire, and crawled into bed. Outside, the Klamath River flowed smooth and wide, stars sleeping on its back.

He slept through the night. The fire died down to a bed of coals. And next morning, as the red sun started rising up, the husband traveled along the trail of the Milky Way, and he never came back.

WHERE KOOMOOKUMPTS SLEEPS

For thousands of years the Modocs have gone on vision quests, sleeping in Koomookumpts' Bed, seeking power. The stone bed, at the top of a rock rising from the desert basin near Tule Lake, is the sacred center of the Modoc world.

It was here that Koomookumpts, Modoc creator, made the world from the water of Tule Lake, reaching five times to scoop mud from the bottom and spreading it around to make the land. He shaped and decorated the world the same way a Modoc woman shapes and decorates a basket. When Koomookumpts was done he crawled into his bed, and his spirit sleeps there still. Here is where the world began and where the visions of her people are created, and where they live on.

These days, Koomookumpts' Bed is also called Petroglyph Point.

When I was eleven, I first visited Lava Beds National Monument near Tule Lake. I was a Boy Scout. The sight of lava flows and volcanoes, marshes and caves and sagebrush and junipers, the night eyes of deer browsing through camp, the hooting of owls under a moon that stared hard and cold onto the desert landscape—these visions slipped into my dreams, leaving pictures in my memory that are vivid to this day.

The initial excitement of that first trip was the campfire ceremony during which we first-year scouts were inducted into the highly secretive Order of the Modocs. But as I crawled through caves and climbed cinder cones, I suspected that the ceremony was a rough imitation of traditions that stretched back further than memory.

As I stared at the quarter mile of ancient symbols carved into the cliff at Koomookumpts' Bed, I had no idea of the mythic significance of the place. I read the sign that dismissed the symbols as graffiti or primitive doodling, standing behind a chain-link fence that did little to protect the carvings from vandals with guns.

I knew there was more to this rock. Eagles and red-tailed hawks lived here, and jackrabbits and deer and coyotes. The carvings seemed as natural a part of the cliff as the nests of owls, and less out of place than the fence and the sign. The symbols meant that Indians had lived here.

For an eleven-year-old Boy Scout, that was good enough for me.

At a time when lake water still lapped the lower cliffs of the rock, a man climbed to the top and had a vision. We know his story because he carved it, using traditional symbols, on a lower cliff that faces east.

As the rising sun is a new beginning for each day, so this man's vision was a new beginning for his life.

He steered his canoe through tules bent over by red-winged blackbirds guarding their nests, past yellow pond lilies the Modocs call wocus. He landed the canoe and started up the ancient trail to the top of the rock.

Once there, he saw that the top was a model of the world. A ring of cliffs circled the rock like mountains, and in the center was a pond. The water was caught in an ancient crater, a memory from when this rock was an underwater volcano and the level of Tule Lake was much higher. But it was also a memory from when the world was nothing but water, before creation.

The man circled the rock, following the cliffs, looking out on the world through gaps, until he came to the pond. He waded through mud toward the center, and then he dove. Five times he struggled to the bottom. On the fifth dive, he swallowed water and imitated

Koomookumpts, scooping mud from the bottom.

The man walked east to the stone bed, lay down, and closed his eyes. And there he remained for five days and five nights. He had no food, no fire, no blankets. And most importantly, he was alone.

The communal thinking of the village, that fluid confusion of primal knowledge and voices and dust, had been left behind. Here the thinking was harder, more intense.

He felt the gnaw of loneliness. A cold wind blurred the sharpness of the stars. The moon lit the nights like a tribal fire. Coyotes howled down the rock. But the man didn't feel the cold. He didn't hear the coyotes. The singing of his heart had taken over. His vision had started.

Thousands of Modocs before him had climbed the rock and slept in Koomookumpts' Bed. One by one they felt the winter wind sting their eyes as they watched coyotes dance in the purple twilight on the frozen surface of Tule Lake.

Thousands before him had felt the shift of the seasons from winter to spring. Rafts of mallards and pelicans and coots replaced the ice on the lake. Snow lines climbed the mountains. The south wind warmed the basin into desert heat.

One by one they climbed the rock as the days cooled into fall. With the first snow, the people gathered around fires in the winter lodges and sang and danced and listened to the myths. The orphan boy Gaukos became the moon. Coyote stole fire for the people. Koomookumpts traveled beyond where the sun and moon live to bring his dead daughter back to the land of the living.

They listened to the stories. Then one by one, through the seasons, through years and centuries, they climbed the rock and listened to the songs of their visions.

Just before dawn on the fifth day, the man's vision cleared. From the top of the rock he saw his village on the south shore of Tule Lake. Dozens of winter lodges covered the basalt-and-sagebrush peninsula that jutted into the water. Smoke rose in thin streams from smoke holes, mixing with layers of morning mist, then spreading south over the rough landscape of lava flows toward volcanoes that would again puff smoke while the Modocs called this village Gumbat, Village Among the Rocks.

The barking of geese started the morning. The sun rose over Koomookumpts' Bed, turning the snow on Mount Shasta orange, spilling into ravines on the eastern ridge. These ravines were the ones Koomookumpts carved with his fingernails so water flowed down the mountains and filled rivers and lakes.

The day moved into the laughter of children, the slow drumming of women pounding wocus seeds into flour in stone bowls, the shouts and bustling of men preparing to hunt. The wind blew the lake surface into waves that bent the reeds on the marshy shore.

Morning burned to midday heat that slowed the pace of village life. In the sluggish rhythm of afternoon, there was no hint that centuries later, US Army troops would build rock fortifications over the mounds and pits of the abandoned village. There was no hint they would attack the last band of Modocs left on their traditional land, nor that the Modoc leader, Kientpuash, Captain Jack, would be imprisoned at Koomookumpts' Bed after his capture, at the same place the Modoc world had started. On that typical afternoon in the village, there was no hint of the strange irony to come—that an ancient lifestyle would come to an end at the rock where it had begun.

The day dimmed toward evening. Under the opening of stars and the rising of the moon, the man started back down the trail. Walking away from the stone bed, his thoughts filled with the lonely memory of his vision and the urge to go home and rejoin the communal rhythms of daily living.

Five days later, the man returned to the rock and carved the story of his experience into the base of the cliff. But his carving did not reveal details of his vision. That would have betrayed the spirit that was to become his power for life. He simply canoed home to his people with the focused eyes of a man who had been touched by the creator and shared his visions.

◇◇◇◇◇

Since that first visit as a Boy Scout, I have returned to Lava Beds season after season, year after year. I have slept in Koomookumpts' Bed and have felt the wind that carved the upper cliffs carve images into my dreams. The pond is dry these days. But one warm night, under a sky blazing with the fire of stars, I walked through the center of the crater and felt cold air surround me with the sharpness of a vision. And I drank the cold air, like water.

WHERE THE
SUN AND MOON LIVE

June twilight brings long shadows to the juniper and sage country around Lower Klamath Lake. To the west, moonlight brushes the snowy summit of Mount Shasta. On the lake, ducks and geese gather into flocks for the night.

Coyote and I wander along the twists of Sheepy Creek near where it flows into the lake. Here is the site of the Old Time village of Shapasheni and, looming behind, the crescent-moon-shaped ridge made famous in Modoc myths as the home of the sun and moon. After lighting the world, the tellers say, the sun and night-sun nap in their lair inside the ridge. When they awake, they travel east underground through lava tubes to rise again and begin their journeys across the sky. My mind whirls with the possibilities of what lurks beyond the shadows of the approaching night. I see some hollow place deep inside the ridge. As I walk, my thoughts are wrapped in the words of ancient myths and the ageless chirping of night critters.

Coyote shatters the magic. "Remind me why we're out here in the middle of nowhere?"

"I'm not sure," I say.

"How encouraging."

"I'll know it when it happens."

"My, you humans are vague. Want something concrete to add to your dreamy meanderings?"

"Like what?"

"I smell smoke."

"Ah, surely it's a sign."

"Right," says Coyote.

I run my eyes along the base of the ridge. Sure enough, from a hidden place tucked in the rocks, the golden glow of a campfire sends a faint glimmer across the shadows, mixing with pale moonlight as it shimmers across the lake.

As we approach, we see a young man sitting by himself. Close up, the fire is full of colors, as if someone caught the palette of the sunset and dropped it into the flames. The colors are muted and rich on the young man's face, and his black eyes shine in the firelight. He stands and waves a welcoming gesture toward Coyote and me. "Lu'lamna," he whispers. "Follow me." He turns from the fire, walks swiftly through a jumble of boulders, and disappears into a cave.

Up for anything that might perk up this trek, Coyote leaps into full energy, lays out his tail, and follows the young man. I am close behind.

At first, it is light inside the cave. Drops of water glisten on the ceiling. Warm air swishes through, and water droplets plop to the floor like stars from the sky just before sunrise. I imagine that the blazing eye of the sun has recently rushed past and left behind a path of light and heat for the lukewarm moon. I struggle to move quickly over the rough floor of the cave. I look ahead. I have lost sight of Coyote and the young man. I listen. The only sounds are dripping water, the whisper of a warm breeze, and my own footsteps. As I walk on, the cave grows darker.

In total darkness, time tells its own story. Outside, days, seasons, and years are defined by risings and settings of the sun, and months by the phases of the moon. Deep in the cave, I might as well be traveling through Mythtime or Dreamtime, where sequences of moments are framed by the telling of stories. At any instant it is possible for world floods to rise and fall as a single bead of water drops from the ceiling, or for centuries to whiz past with a few words whispered in darkness. It is no surprise that the sun and moon travel through this cave as they prepare to tell those living on the outside that another day is about to begin.

Beyond my musings of time, this cave has genuine harshness. If this is the underground path of the sun and moon, this journey is different for them than their travels across the sky. This cave has twists and turns. There are blind corners that are best to peer around before walking ahead, and side caverns that are rocky crossroads fraught with decisions. A wrong choice might send one groping down a pitch-black passage where the air smells stale and one stumbles over scatterings of old bones that litter the floor. This journey is not the graceful, open-air arcs the sun and moon make across the sky. In the deepest parts of the cave, travel is slow, tentative, uncertain. Here the sun and moon experience a daily drama of earth-bound existence up close.

After several stumbles and one good head-bang on a low ceiling sharp with basalt, I am about to turn back when I see a glimmer of light ahead. I turn a corner and find Mister Coyote crouched in a side opening of the cave.

"Shhh," whispers Coyote. "He's resting."

Across a jumble of rocks, I see the young man sitting quietly, gazing at the sky. He sits on a flat boulder in the shape of a natural chair. I look around. I know this place. Symbol Bridge. Many times I have walked the desert trail to visit the rock paintings. There are dozens, and one of them shows the sun traveling through a cave.

As I watch the young man, the light grows and the first sunlight of the day slips over the rock rim and finds its way into the cave. The young man leans forward. His gaze is intense. He points toward the sky. Something is different. I walk out of the cave and look skyward. All of the stars have disappeared in the bright light of the morning except one, and it shines as bright in the daytime sky as it did at night.

A supernova, I'm thinking, like the explosion that created the Crab Nebula. In 1054, the Modocs saw this star in the daytime sky for months. They painted pictures of it here at Symbol Bridge and a few miles away, in Fern Cave. As I run this through my mind, the young man is busy adding new symbols to the cave wall: a rising sun, a bright star, a crescent moon … When he's finished, he disappears into the cave. Coyote leaps into action, trailing the young man.

As I walk past the stone chair, I see no sign that the young man was ever there. No drops of fresh paint, and the only symbols on the cave wall are the ancient ones I have visited many times. Nothing looks different. I walk back into the cave. The path is smooth, clear of rocks, and I hustle to catch up with Coyote.

"Parts of this cave aren't on the maps, you know."

"That makes it the best kind of cave, doesn't it?" says Coyote.

"And the symbols he painted a few minutes ago have been there for centuries."

"That makes this journey even more interesting."

"So what's the deal?" I ask. "Are we in a story or a dream?"

"What a question for a storyteller to ask," says Coyote. "I thought we worked through this a few stories back."

"Well, are we? You're the expert."

"I dunno," says Coyote. "Looks like a cave to me."

Coyote pushes all four legs into a trot and disappears into the darkness.

At the next cave entrance I see several folks gathered in the faint light. As Coyote disappears into the crowd, I yell to him, "Hey, Coyote, what time is it?"

It's a silly question to toss at Coyote, of course, but it is the first thing I can think of. I want Coyote's attention. I'm surprised when he answers, "It's four-thirty a.m. on the summer solstice!"

"What year?"

"Doesn't matter!"

It matters to me. I recognize the rock painting near the cave entrance. It interacts with the rising sun to mark the longest day of the year. I also know that an earthquake a few years back shifted the rock that focuses the sunlight onto the wall next to the painting, and it hasn't worked since. I scratch my head.

"Why are people here?" I ask myself. "There's nothing to see."

I remember the words of the Modoc elder who first led me to this place. "Each year in June, the Old Ones say, there is a time in our calendar when the sun and moon and an ancient rock writing combine their powers to herald the coming of the warm days, days that ripen the gooseberries, days that green the marsh around Tule Lake and fill our world with the heat of the summer sun and the warmth of moonlight."

Recalling the first time I witnessed this event, I speak the words of my own story softly to myself …

Before sunrise, the sky was brilliant, not from the rising sun—though there was a faint wash of color in the east—but with the light of the moon, which rose full the night before. Through clumps of sagebrush and shadows of tall pines, mule deer crisscrossed our camp and owls talked from treetop to treetop, telling stories of last night's good hunting under the moon.

I was camped with friends on the forested edge of the desert basin. From an owl's view, the basin looked huge in the early morning. Tule Lake was shadowed smooth, spotted with flocks of dozing geese and pelicans and coots.

As the shadows shifted and the eastern light turned orange, we were already in the rig driving toward a solstice rock writing, where each year the sun reaffirmed the circling of the seasons, an event that has happened since the Old Time, when the Human People and the Animal People were not so different and Coyote was just getting known in this place.

As we bumped along the road, I thought of last night's moonrise. From our camp behind a cinder cone without a view of the basin, the rising came late. Obscuring the moon was a bulk of clouds shaped like a bear. Frustrated at the thought of missing the moonrise, I improvised a Modoc chant. In the best Coyote voice I could muster, I screamed it out. The trees bounced the chant through the forest until the multitude of echoes sounded like an entire tribe of Coyote People.

"Hey hey hey hey hey! Frog in the moon, do you hear me? Can't you see

Bear is swallowing your home? We like looking at the moon and seeing you watching our world. So listen—hey hey hey hey Frog! Let loose on Bear's nose. Water his nose with your juice. Make him stop swallowing your home. Come on, Frog, we like seeing you! Hey hey hey hey hey!"

It must have worked. Clouds shrank into the trees. Bear went back to his lodge in the stars. The moon rose huge and white, the dark shape of Frog grinning away. The night stayed clear, no rain—Frog didn't miss and water our camp!—and I went to sleep under the light of the moon, with the coming light of the solstice sunrise in my dreams.

By the time we arrived at the cave the moon was going down, leaving a trace of color, and there were several cars parked along the road. We walked the short trail past an ancient cairn and scrambled down rocks to the cave entrance. It was near sunrise, and we stood staring at the painted symbols that have come to be called the Solstice Pictograph.

An elder translated the message. "At this place, on the longest day of the year, the sun will rise over the eastern hills and shine freely, just to the right of the cave entrance."

As light began to spread across the basin, the sun rose orange over the curve of the hills to the east, making the tops of a dozen cinder cones glow like fire. People gathered and watched the rock face to the left of the symbols. A few minutes after sunrise, the sun streamed between rocks and formed a fist of sunlight on the rock face. Over the next several minutes, a finger grew from the fist and moved down the rock, past the symbols, until it pointed directly to a crack that resembled the cave itself. Less than an hour later, the fist and finger disintegrated into a mass of sunlight, spilled into the crack, and was gone.

The crowd of people, many of them unimpressed, walked back to their cars and drove down the road. We stayed on and took in the wonder of the day. More shapes of sunlight traveled the rock face. With the crowd gone, the day turned quiet. The morning breeze made the same swishing sound the sun and moon might make traveling through the cave, or the sound of the sun rising and walking west across the sky.

We spent all day watching sunlight and shadows and sharing stories. Near sunset, I walked to where my friends stood at the cairn.

"Hey, Doty! Look at this! Stand here. Put your heels against this rock and look at the sun."

My heels fit perfectly into a groove. It was worn, as if many people over thousands of years had stood here. The cairn was directly in front of me, and the sun was going down in a splash of color over a distant cinder cone, directly over the dip in the crater. This was a perfect alignment: myself, the cairn, the cinder cone, and the sun traveling toward Shapasheni.

In the gathering darkness, we sat near the cairn and looked over the desert basin, waiting for the moon to rise. The air was cool, the desert heat of the day staying on only in the rocks. The green marsh around Tule Lake was in shadow. Mule deer browsed in the open, and owls predicted with vivid voices their nighttime hunting. I went back over the past night and day in my head. The sun and moon had acted out their yearly ritual, and I had been part of the ceremony, at home in this ancient place where the sun and moon live their lives.

"Hey, Doty!" yells Coyote. "Are you coming?"

"Where did everyone go?"

"Who are you talking about?"

"All those people."

"You're nuts! It's just me and you."

"Right. Where's the young man?"

"He went into the cave. We'd better hurry."

"Did the fist of sunlight work?"

"Of course," says Coyote. "It always works for me!"

In the middle of the night the stars are brilliant from the top of Petroglyph Point, a rock near the eastern shore of Tule Lake that was once an underwater volcano. Coyote and I emerge out of the cave near the base of the rock, along the old shoreline of the lake, and we walk up the old Indian trail to the summit. We find the young man sitting on a stone bench in the center of the rock. I sit down next to him.

Coyote surveys the top of the rock, the ring of cliffs around the edge, the slope toward the small crater in the center. He leaps into the open. "Hey, look at this place! A natural amphitheater. Just right for a one-dog show!"

Coyote struts in the starlight. "Now, a long, long time ago, Coyote Old Man—that's me wearing one of my nifty masks—made the world. He reached deep into the water of the lake and scooped up mud and spread it around to make the land. Then he made the sun and moon, and the days and nights, and he placed all the stars just so in the sky. He named the seasons, and he scattered lesser critters called people around until they were as many as stars. They spent centuries telling stories about Coyote the Creator, Coyote the Bringer of Life, Coyote the Eternal Howl of Wisdom …"

A woman's voice drifts out of the night sky. "Not quite right, Mister Teller of Tall Tales."

Coyote sticks his nose into the air. "Who are you, and what have you got to do with it?"

"I'm your mother, and I was there."

"Oh, oh," says Coyote, and he slinks over to the bench and sits down next to me and the young man.

"Now pay attention, you little pip-squeak puppy, and maybe you'll learn something. This is how it happened …"

Voices begin whispering among the stars until there is a chorus of storytellers acting out the beginning of the Modoc world.

Koomookumpts says: It was me who made the world from the mud of Tule Lake.

Coyote's Mother says: After that, Koomookumpts became the sun. He built a lodge called Shapasheni, far to the west. He rested there after long hours of traveling the sky and spreading light across the world.

Koomookumpts says: I called a great Council of Mythological Beings, and we made lots of decisions about how the world ought to be. We decided the lengths of the day and night and how the people should live.

Coyote wanted the winter to be twelve months long. Everyone thought that was a bad idea, so we made it three months and made other seasons for the rest of the year. We put Mister Bear in charge of the seasons. He built his lodge among the stars, and the people call him Great Bear in the Sky.

Gaukos says: Since I was an orphan anyway, I agreed to be the moon.

Coyote's Mother says: Gaukos came to visit me in my lodge. I made him twenty-four masks to make him bright and beautiful. One mask covered another, and when he removed one, there was a new month. But one day Koomookumpts stopped by when I wasn't there, and that no-good son of mine showed him the masks.

Koomookumpts says: Like mother, like son, I said. Twenty-four masks was too long a year. There was no way the people would survive the winters. So I honored the decision of the council and smashed half of the masks. I went back to the council and told everyone that the world was ready for people.

Water Snake says: I wanted people to shed their skins like I do and be young forever.

Mole says: I said the world would get too crowded.

Koomookumpts says: Everyone agreed that people should grow old, get cold, and sit down and shake and die. And that's just what they started doing. That council lasted for five days and was a lot of work, so when I was done I went to sleep in my stone bed, right where you are sitting. From that day on, the Old Ones called this rock Koomookumpts' Bed. It is the center of our universe. One of these days I'll wake up and put the world back the way it used to be.

Coyote's Mother says: A white owl glides across the top of the rock and lands on the cliff above the stone bed. The rock face is covered with ancient carvings that tell the story of the Modoc world. When they are young, girls and boys come here to seek visions and become complete people. Near the end of their lives, they gaze at this rock where Koomookumpts made the world and are reminded how their own lives began.

Owl says: The roof of my lodge is the night sky. I see all the stars and I listen to their stories. Sometimes a star streaks across the sky and falls to the earth, and I hear him whisper the name of someone who is about to die. I speak the name back so everyone knows. Where the star falls is where the death will happen. Many shooting stars means many people will die.

Voices from Far Away say: We are traveling toward the Land of the Dead, beyond that mountain to the west. Our path is the Milky Way. You can see our campfires at night as we camp along the trail. In the daytime we run so fast you cannot see us.

Coyote's Mother says: Owl flies into the night. His white shape shrinks to the size of a star and disappears into the haze of the Milky Way. The crescent moon clears the ridge and sends a sliver of light across the rock. Shouting comes from the moon.

Frog Woman says: Hey, knock it off!

Great Bear in the Sky says: Who, me?

Frog Woman says: Yes, you! Every night you take another bite out of Gaukos. Just mention your name and the poor fellow starts shaking. We've had enough moon phases for this month. Go home and do your dance and keep the seasons moving. I'm the wife of Gaukos, and I have special powers. Stick around here and you'll be sorry!

Great Bear in the Sky says: All right, all right, just for tonight.

Coyote's Mother says: Bear returns to his home. He lights a fire and North Star blazes. He dances a circle dance to his left, and the night air turns warm on this first night of summer. The moon travels across the sky as he dances through the night.

Morning Star says: Better hurry this story along. It's almost daytime, and I need to give the sun a morning nudge.

Coyote's Mother says: Coyote stands up and stamps his foot.

Coyote says: What about me? Surely I do more.

Coyote's Mother says: The star Capella flashes colors just above the horizon to the north. She is known among the people as Coyote's Star.

Coyote's Star says: Ooooo, Coyote. Yes, you did a lot more. You're a fool of a dog, you know. One night you danced with me to the top of the sky.

Coyote says: Oh, oh, I remember that. You dumped me! That hurt, and it took me a long time to gather up my parts and put myself back together.

Coyote's Mother says: Maybe so, but Crater Lake formed in the mountain where you crash-landed. That lake is a place of dreams and power and stories, and the best deep mirror of our world we could ever ask for.

Morning Star says: That's all for tonight. Ningadaniak. This story is finished.

Coyote's Mother says: Between night and day there is a deep silence as each storyteller draws a new breath.

"Not much of a one-dog show, was it?" I say.

"Humph," says Coyote. He curls up in the stone bed, closes his eyes, and is soon dreaming heroic stories about himself.

I look around. The young man is gone. "Who was he? Some lunar deity out of Mythtime? Perhaps Aisis, the son of Koomookumpts? Maybe he was just some regular guy who knew the way."

Coyote half opens an eye. "He wasn't even there. You just thought you needed a guide. He's part of the mythological fireworks that live in your brain. Your own mental supernova."

"Imagined? Like you?"

"Right," says Coyote, and he's back asleep.

I shake my head and free myself from questions that have no answers. I walk a little ways from the stone bed, where I can see east through a gap in the cliff. I hear the chatter of geese as they rise off the lake. I watch the sun rise bright into the summer sky. It looks like a giant eye, wide open. I glance west and see the crescent moon, an eye closing as it heads toward sleep at Shapasheni. I imagine the view of the universe the sun and moon have, a dramatic eye-opener after their dark travels through the cave.

I stand on the cliff-edge at the center of the world and whisper the words from a Modoc song.

"Sun and Night-Sun, you know everything. You see me night and day. Give me your eyes that I may see as you do. You have given me much. You warm me on a cold day. You make all that is my food. You light the day and night. You make the seasons. Sun and Night-Sun, you know everything. You are over me night and day. Give me your eyes that I may see as you do."

AT THEIR BEST, STORIES HEAL

OUR NATIVE LITERATURE COMES IN TWO FORMS: stories told, and stories written with symbols, carved or painted on rocks, on wood, on bone, or woven into baskets. Everything is passed along through stories. If you want to understand native people, listen to our stories. Or read the rocks. Muse on a basket. That's the way we've been learning about ourselves for centuries.

The rock writing symbol for communication is two heads connected by a line, the original talking heads! Line up the heads and walk in that direction to find more symbols. You might be led to a cliff with symbols that give directions to a good water source or a nearby village. You might be led to a cave. Walk inside to find dozens of symbols that tell the native story of this place.

The stories we tell each other entertain us on those long winter nights. But they do more than that. They teach us many things about our culture, our history, our folklore, our beliefs. Even practical things, like how to build a house or where to find huckleberries in the mountains or the best fishing places along the river. But stories do even more. When they are doing their best work, stories heal. A skilled storyteller can make us feel better about things we might not be feeling too good about. Stories touch us deeply where we feel our emotions, and they stay with us for a long time. Doctors know this. So do therapists, ministers, teachers. And so do storytellers. Some of the rock writings are located at native places of healing.

The best way to understand the healing power of storytelling is to tell you a story about a student who found her story.

A number of years ago I was Storyteller in Residence at a school on the Oregon coast. My first day was also a 4th-grade girl's first day. She had moved from eastern Oregon—a huge change of environment from the desert to the coast—and not only was she going through the usual new-kid-in-school traumas, she had it doubly hard. The girl had long, skinny legs, and from her first day, the students teased her. These were the same children she had hoped to make friends with. This made her sad.

While in one of my workshops, she composed a story she asked to perform for the entire class. This was not a requirement for the workshop. We were working in small groups. Each storyteller's first performance would be for a small audience of friends. But the girl insisted. This took courage. She mustered up her nerve, and the story had an amazing impact on her classmates.

Her story was about Crane, a large bird with skinny legs, and how the other animals teased her. "This isn't right," thought Crane. "I shouldn't be judged by how I look." Crane decided to show the other animals that there was more to her than skinny legs.

In her story was a river, and the animals wanted to see what was on the other side. But the river was too deep to wade, too swift to swim, and this was before boats and bridges, even before birds had wings.

One day, Crane stretched one of her skinny legs across the river. She made the first bridge, and the animals walked across. But no animals teased Crane. They knew she might start shaking her leg when they were halfway across at the deepest and swiftest part of the river, dump them in, and that would be their end!

As the girl told her story, the class was dead quiet. The truth of the story, the moral, the theme, the meaning, the power, the wisdom, the teaching—don't judge people!—came across loud and clear. Then the bell rang. Her classmates went to recess.

Out on the playground, an amazing thing happened. Oral tradition happened. The students who had heard the story told it to those who hadn't, and just like stories have been spreading around for thousands of years, that story spread all through the school. By the end of the day, nearly all of the students had quit teasing her. Within a week, she had some good friends.

That's what I call a healing story ... a little something to make the world a better place.

PANTHER AND THE
WHITE DUCK WOMEN

Native people of the West have been water people for a long time. Boats are common in ancient myths. In a Takelma story, the White Duck sisters paddle across the sea from the Village Beyond the Sunset to the Rogue River. In another story, Coyote refuses to be ferried across the river to the Land of the Dead. At a sacred island in Tule Lake, a quarter mile of ancient stories were carved into a shoreline cliff by people standing in boats. Since that mythic time when the world was nothing but water, native waterways have been well traveled.

Along the Rogue River, the people tell this story.

The oak leaves along the river were gold, glowing in the sun, all fluttering and waving in the wake of the fall breezes.

Panther and his younger brother, Wildcat, lived in a plank house where the river rushed like the wind. And downriver, on the other side, where the river slowed and gathered fog, Coyote and his mother lived in a poor house made of bark. Inside the house, it was cold and damp. There was no fire. Coyote hadn't bothered to gather any wood.

Panther spent the days hunting, bringing home plenty of deer. His younger brother worked long hours drying the meat, filling the house with deer meat for the coming winter. The fall sun shone at Panther's house. The fire burned warm inside, sending breezes of smoke out the smoke hole.

Far to the west, across the ocean, in the Village Beyond the Sunset, people told stories of how good a hunter Panther was. Two young women who were living at the village started on a journey. They were sisters, and people called them White Duck Women.

They left their home one morning when the rising sun shone warm and gold, and they paddled across the ocean to the mouth of the Rogue River. They started walking upriver into the fog. They were going to find Panther and marry him. As they neared Coyote's house, the fog was so thick they could hardly see the trail.

They had heard plenty of stories about Coyote back in their village, stories that had been told for years and years. Before they started, an elder of the village told them, "Stay away from that one. He's full of tricks, and you can't trust anything he says."

Coyote was pulling bark off trees when he heard them coming.

"What should I do?" he asked himself.

Now, Coyote kept tapeworms as pets, and he was always asking them for advice. He sat under the tree and said to his tapeworms, "There are two good-looking women coming toward my house. What should I do?"

The largest tapeworm said, "Now, that depends what you want to get out of the situation."

The middle-sized tapeworm said, "We all know what Coyote wants. A couple of wives to do all his work. He's such a lazy lout."

"I don't like the way you two are talking."

The smallest tapeworm spoke up. "Say, Coyote, why don't you turn that bark you're peeling into planks? Make a nice-looking house for a change. Spruce up your reputation a bit. Those women will be very impressed."

That gave Coyote an idea. He ran to his house and covered the bark with planks. He brought his mother a stone bowl and pounding stone, hung fancy beads on her dress, and told her to sit and pound acorns into flour.

He said, "Now listen, you old bat. When these two women come here, don't say a word. Just pound acorns and keep your trap shut."

Coyote scampered back down the trail through the fog. He sat down and waited for the White Duck Women.

As they got closer, Coyote could see their shapes in the fog, and he liked how they walked. They walked up to Coyote, and he said, "Hello, friends. Is there anything I can help you with?"

The elder sister said, "We are traveling to Panther's house. Do you know where he lives?"

"Why, this is your lucky day. I am Panther. I'm the one you're looking for."

The White Duck Women stared hard at him through the fog. The younger sister started sniffing. She nudged her elder sister and whispered, "That is not Panther. That one is Coyote. Look at his ragged tail and his ribs poking out. A good hunter wouldn't have ribs like that. And just take a whiff. Phew! That one's Coyote, for sure!"

But the elder sister said, "No, you are wrong. This must be Panther."

Coyote said, "My house is just up the trail. It's a fancy plank house, the nicest one around."

Without saying another word, the White Duck Women walked upriver through the fog to Coyote's house.

They went inside. It was cold and damp. There was no fire. Coyote's mother sat in one corner, pounding acorns.

They hadn't been inside long when the younger sister said, "Old woman, could you tell us where Panther's house is? We are looking for Panther."

Coyote's mother stopped pounding. "Upriver, on the other side, that is where Panther lives. He lives in a nice house. He and his younger brother work pretty hard. He's not lazy like my own son."

The White Duck Women thanked her and continued upriver. They paddled across the river, and as they got near Panther's house, the sun was shining. The river crashed over rocks and logs, crashing and crashing like the waves at their own village.

Coyote came back through the fog to his house. He went inside and said to his mother, "Well, where have your daughters-in-law gone?"

Coyote's mother said, "What are you talking about? I have no daughters-in-law. Who would want to marry you?"

"Those two good-looking girls came here to marry me. Where have they gone?"

"Those two? Not them! I sent them on upriver. They didn't come here for you. They were looking for Panther."

Coyote got steaming mad. He lunged at his mother, grabbed her by the neck, and strangled her. Then he threw her into the dead fire pit and covered her with old ashes.

He rushed out of the house, swam the river, and chased after the White Duck Women, upriver, toward the place where the sun was shining.

Back in the fog, Coyote's mother sang as she rolled in the ashes, bringing herself back to life.

Coyote caught up with them just before they reached Panther's house. He jumped around, screaming, "Now you two won't be young anymore! You'll be nothing but old women!"

When the White Duck Women arrived at Panther's house, they looked old. Their basket caps were worn out, their teeth gone, their faces wrinkled, and they carried walking sticks to help them along.

They went inside. Wildcat was sitting in one corner, drying deer meat. But Panther wasn't there. He was hunting.

The White Duck Women sat by the fire and waited for Panther to come home.

It was evening when Panther came home with the deer he had killed. The sun went down in a blaze of red and orange, and the stars came out, lighting the sky.

When he went inside, he took one look at the White Duck Women sitting in the warm blaze of the fire, and he said to his younger brother,

"Wildcat, these must be our grandmothers. They have come here to visit. Give them soft food to eat. Give them deer liver."

The White Duck Women, looking old and weary, feasted on liver until everyone curled up near the fire and went to sleep.

Next morning, and all day long, Panther hunted deer. Wildcat stayed home and prepared food for the winter. And the White Duck Women made themselves useful by gathering and pounding acorns.

Four days went by, clear fall days, the sun shining bright, the river crashing downriver below the house, and Wildcat giving the White Duck Women plenty of soft liver to eat.

On the fifth day, the White Duck Women were pounding acorns outside the house in the warm sun, and they looked older than ever, wrinkled and bent over.

When they were done with the pounding, they started to leach the flour through river water in a basket. Some of the water dripped on the elder sister's hand and turned it all smooth, without wrinkles.

"Oh, younger sister, look here. Look what the water has done to my hand!"

The elder White Duck Woman rushed down to the river and put her whole arm into the water, and it was all smooth and young again. She splashed into the water, into the flow of the river, and came out on the other side, young and pretty.

Her sister followed behind. They both bathed in the river, letting the swift water come up all around them, and they went back to being young again. They swam back across the river, climbed the bank, and went back into Panther's house, taking the acorn flour with them.

They made acorn soup for Wildcat and said to him, "Your brother Panther has been calling us your grandmothers for a long time now. But we really came here to marry him. We were young then, like we are now. But Coyote did us wrong. Now we are going away, downriver toward our home."

The White Duck Women left Panther's house and started their

long journey. They didn't cross over the river until they were well past Coyote's house.

Wildcat climbed onto the roof and called out, "Oh, elder brother, your wives have gone away! Come back, elder brother, your wives have left!"

When Panther got back to the house, Wildcat told him the whole story. Panther went to one corner of the house and took a string of dentalium shells and strung them across the house. Then he stood a rock acorn pounder up and said to Wildcat, "I am going now. If this string of shells breaks or the pounder falls, you will know that I have been killed."

He went out of the house and started downriver.

The days were moving into winter, cloudy and cold, and the wind had blown all the oak leaves off the trees and scattered them every which way. They littered the banks of the Rogue River, dead and brown.

Panther kept a fast pace, and soon he saw the White Duck Women ahead of him. He took his bow, fitted an arrow, and shot it over their heads. But the White Duck Women did not look back. They picked up the arrow and put it in one of their baskets. Again Panther shot an arrow. And again they put it away without looking behind them.

They were getting close to the ocean. The wind blew hard, and the fog was thick, full of salt and the crashing of the sea.

When the White Duck Women arrived at the mouth of the river, Panther caught up with them. They talked to one another, and the White Duck Women called Panther their husband. They brought him a canoe to paddle on the journey across the ocean to their home, the Village Beyond the Sunset.

But the elder sister warned him, "Do not look into the water, even though you hear voices from below. Whatever you do, do not look into the sea."

The White Duck Women started paddling across, and Panther followed in his canoe. The wind was blowing. Mist swirled over the top of the water. When they reached the breakers, the White Duck Women were feeling close to their home. Panther was feeling at home as well, thinking, "These waves sound just like the river where it rushes along below my own home."

They went through the breakers and into the open sea. Panther followed behind. It was feeling less like home to him now, the wind whipping the surf into spray, soaking him to the bone. The mist was so thick he could hardly see the women ahead of him. He was thinking of the warm fire back at his house and a good meal of deer meat.

Then the voices started, rising through the spray: "Ugly-mug Panther. Cat eater. Claw foot."

Panther was getting mad. He hissed to himself, trying to keep from looking into the water.

The wind tossed the voices around his head: "Lazy hunter. Stink tail. Vomit face!"

That last one had done it. Panther couldn't stand it any longer. He grabbed his bow, fitted an arrow, leaned over the side of the canoe, looking and looking through the mist and the spray into the water. But before he saw a thing, a giant head burst through the surface, hollow eyes filled with sea mist, the mouth opening wider than wide, and with a whistling, sucking noise, swallowed down Panther, canoe and all.

Then there was nothing but the wind and the ocean and the foam.

Wildcat was sitting inside by the fire listening to the winter wind blow across the smoke hole when he heard the string of dentalium shells snap and the rock acorn pounder fall over and break into pieces. And he knew that his brother was dead.

He crawled onto the roof of the house and sat in the cold wind, crying and crying:

> hae-aye-bee-yae
> hae-aye-bee-yae
> hae-aye-bee-yae

o-bee-ya

o-bee-ya

The wind got stronger and blew Wildcat off the roof, but he crawled
back up and wailed:

alas, o elder brother

alas, o elder brother

alas, o elder brother

o elder brother

o elder brother

For hours and hours Wildcat sang his brother's death song. Then,
exhausted, he went back inside the house. The fire had gone out a long
while before. He dug into the fire pit, put aside the ashes, and he crawled
in, curling up like a dog. He stayed there for a long time, listening to
the wind:

hae-aye-bee-yae

o-bee-ya

When the White Duck Women reached the Village Beyond the
Sunset, the ocean was smooth and the sun was shining like it was spring.
A warm breeze blew, and the people of the village were sitting outside.

They paddled through the waves onto the beach and looked behind
them. No Panther. They waited a while, looking and looking, but
Panther wasn't anywhere to be seen. They only saw the cloud of foam
and mist and winter wind where it roared across the sea.

They called to their friends, "Our husband. He is lost. Someone come
help us."

Many people gathered on the beach. It was decided that the best thing
would be to try diving for Panther where the White Duck Women had
last seen him.

They all paddled into the ocean, toward the place where the wind was blowing the sea wild. Many people dived, looking for a sign of Panther, but no one could reach the bottom. The water was too rough. They got down a certain distance, then floated back up. After many dives they had to give it up. They paddled back to the Village Beyond the Sunset.

When they got there, they saw someone sitting on the beach in the sunlight, weaving a basket. It was Mudcat Woman, and she wasn't weaving any ordinary basket. She wove this one out of sunrays. As sunrays moved across the ocean and shone into the water, she reached out from the place where she was sitting on the beach, grabbed them, and twined them into her basket. Her basket was getting finished quickly, and it glowed with the fresh warmth of a spring day.

The people gathered around her and asked, "What kind of a basket is that?" and "Will it help to find Panther?"

"I can get close to him," she said in a soft voice. "All of you just floated up, but I can get close to him."

The people urged her on, telling her to hurry or Panther might be lost forever. But she would not move until she had the basket finished. She kept saying, "I can get close to him."

At sundown, as the last sunlight hit the water, the basket was done.

Mudcat Woman stood up and walked into the ocean. She waded through the breakers and disappeared under the water, carrying her basket of sunlight. As nighttime floated over their village, the people watched the sun-glow from Mudcat Woman's basket grow fainter as it gained depth below the waves.

The White Duck Women went to their house. They sat inside by the fire. They didn't eat and they didn't speak. They sat staring at the red flames of the fire for a long time.

Mudcat Woman swam below the waves through the darkness, the basket of sunlight making a torch to light her way. She swam through the wavering seaweed, past huge sea rocks covered with white shells that shone like stars in the darkness, past underwater caves where glowing eyes stared out at her. She swam where the depths of the ocean started rocking, and the underwater currents of wind blew the green and yellow plants into a dance, and the huge underwater trees swayed, and the water turned cold, as if winter had blown itself to the bottom of the sea.

She swam on until she came to the cave of the sea monster, the one who had swallowed up Panther. She could see the monster from the entrance, coiled like a serpent, his head on the floor of the cave, sleeping, though his eyes were half open. She swam like the current past those eyes to where Panther's bones were lying in a heap. She put them in her basket and swam out of the cave, away through the swaying ocean forest, out of the cold depths of winter, away toward the village. And the sea monster slept on in his cave.

As Mudcat Woman came out of the water, the sun was coming up, sending its warmth across the sand. People were waiting there.

"Look!" someone shouted. "There she is!"

Mudcat Woman walked across the beach to the sweat house and went inside. People helped to heat the rocks, and Mudcat Woman dripped water on them. The steam started rising, and the air inside the sweat house got hotter and hotter.

Mudcat Woman set the basket of sunlight near the heated stones. The twining still glowed and cast a warm light across Panther's bones. Mudcat Woman sat in the sweat house, singing and chanting, for several days. On the morning of the fifth day, she went outside.

It was just before sunrise. She sat on the beach by herself and sang to the ocean and the sun and the coming spring.

After a while, there was a noise inside the sweat house. The door pushed open, and Panther stood in the morning light, looking like he had always looked.

Early the next morning, Panther and the White Duck Women left the Village Beyond the Sunset and traveled back across the ocean and upriver toward Panther's house.

"Perhaps by now," Panther was thinking, "my younger brother has thrown himself into the river."

They went upriver into the foggy place where Coyote lived. Across the river they could hear him pacing around and talking to himself. "When is that ugly-faced Panther going to get tired of those haggy women? It's been a hundred days! I'm an important person. I can't wait forever."

From inside Coyote's house, a voice whispered, "Important? Maybe. But not so very clever …"

Panther and the White Duck Women went on out of the fog. The sun was shining. A warm breeze was blowing. As they got closer to Panther's house they heard the crashing river, and they all felt they were coming home, the river roaring into their hearts.

When they got to Panther's house, there wasn't any smoke coming out of the smoke hole. They went inside. The fire was dead. Panther went over to the fire pit and found his younger brother, Wildcat, curled up in the ashes.

"Oh, my younger brother. You are dead from grief! My wives, take him to the river and wash the soot off him."

The White Duck Women carried Wildcat down the bank and bathed him in the river.

Panther sat inside his house, his thoughts turning sadder and sadder. As he listened to the spring breeze blow across the smoke hole, his ear caught a voice blowing past. "O elder brother," it was saying. "O elder brother!"

Panther went to the door and looked down at the river. And there was Wildcat, waving to him and climbing back toward his house.

Panther and Wildcat and the White Duck Women lived on at Panther's house. Panther brought home many deer, and everyone worked to keep the house filled with food. The sun shone bright. The Rogue River crashed below. The oak trees sprouted new leaves and turned the world green. And downriver, in the fog and the cold, Coyote kept counting the days as the breezes spun the seasons, scattering words that seemed to grow out of the fog, "Coyote, important? So they say. But sometimes he's not so very clever …"

LONG WALK HOME

ALL NIGHT, WHILE PEOPLE ARE SLEEPING, THEIR shadows are out having a good time. They visit friends. They dance in the woods. Shadows swim in the river. In the morning, people call their shadows back to them. They can't live without their shadows. When I call for my shadow, I say: "Shadow, come home. The sun is nearly here. Come over the mountains. Come home through the valleys. Come home through the morning mist. Cross over the rivers and creeks. Come spend the day with me. I want to live a long time. Shadow, come home."

Nothing is left of the houses at the Takelma village of Ti'lomikh. Not a trace. Nothing to come home to. And yet it feels like home. I have known this mile-long sacred stretch of soil since I was a child. Growing up, I was told stories of the centuries of visitors who found their way along the Rogue River to Ti'lomikh. Imagine this in the mists of Mythtime: the Dragonfly brothers meet Coyote here. Soon after that, the people arrive. Hapkemnas, the creator, shows them how to build houses. This begins a happy village life cycle that lasts for thousands of years.

In 1827, the river brings another visitor, Peter Skene Ogden, a Hudson's Bay fur trapper. A few months earlier, he visits the Modoc village of Gumbat and writes in his journal: "We took the liberty of demolishing their huts for fire wood. I should certainly regret that our side should cause a quarrel with these Indians, for so far their conduct toward us has been certainly most correct and orderly and worthy of imitation by all." He leaves Ti'lomikh intact, but his visit marks the blip in time when the concept of home begins to be redefined by people new to the neighborhood. More come in a flood. Fifty years later, following a bloody war for sod, the original people are gone, forced to make new homes on reservations up north.

Yet Ti'lomikh still feels like home. Native people know that the village is more than the houses and graveyards that define its boundaries. It is a story told by Mother Landscape, the sound of the river, the smell of pines. It is the old man who sits in the stone chair above the falls, watching the first spring salmon swimming up the Rogue River. Weeks before, he had seen their shadows leaping the falls, and he knew they were coming. The river is the lifeblood of the world, the wind her breath. The old man feels the breeze made by the power of the falls. The world is alive, and this is what home is all about.

This is the story I want to find. How do I reassemble the fragments that remain? How do I step outside the outrages of history and live in a time that makes sense? Hapkemnas is my neighbor. Mother Landscape is the village storyteller. The Salmon People stop by for a visit. How do I find my way into the essence of this story?

Simple. I tell Coyote. Seriously. And here's what happens: Not long after, in the middle of the night, he startles me out of bed with his signature howl. He convinces me that significant lessons in mythic time travel are mine for the grabbing. After some dickering, I agree to hire him as my guide and to follow his instructions. Before sunrise, we arrive at Ti'lomikh. We stand on the riverbank and wait for the first light.

This is a quiet moment that has not changed for centuries, this slow transition from darkness to light. Millions of stars give way to one giant star that blazes a path through the morning, eventually finding its way to the village.

"It's time," says Coyote. "Let's head home. We'll take the scenic tour."

Coyote and I walk into the nearby town of Gold Hill and board the Greyhound bus. Sunlight brushes the hills and ridges above the river. The bus jerks into motion, crawls out of town, and rumbles downriver along Highway 99.

"Remind me again why we're riding this bus to Siletz?" I ask.

"So we can walk back."

"That's what I thought. It's a few hundred miles, you know."

"That's right. But you might find walking with us mythic folks is a little different. We cover a lot of distance in less time than you humans, and we see more along the way. Reality is so boring. Remember you promised to trust me on this one?"

"I remember. So, Mister Magical Mythtime, can you get this Greyhound to trot a little faster?"

"I don't mess with domestic dogs. Grandmother is patient. She'll wait for us to get there."

"Of course. So tell me about your grandmother. You've never mentioned her."

"I've always had a grandmother. Grandmother Coyote. Don't you listen to the stories you tell?"

"Sometimes I forget that you claim to be all of the coyotes in the stories: Mister Coyote, Coyote Old Man, Sleuth Hound Coyote, Troublemaker Coyote, Harebrained Coyote …"

"Don't you forget it!"

"It seems that your many incarnations never do. And now your grandmother wants to walk from the reservation to her homeland. A sort of reverse replay of the Trail of Tears? Think she can make it? How old is she?"

"She's as old as I am. We Coyotes never age or get feeble. We simply endure."

"Being a storyteller, I suppose I have myself to thank for that."

"Right again. Wow, you're like this bus."

"How so?"

"You're slow, but you're on a roll!"

This is enough banter for me. I turn and gaze out the window.

The Rogue River appears to flow faster as we travel downstream. The landscape whirs by at highway speeds, even though the bus gets tired and stops to rest at every doughnut shop in every small town. River and highway part ways, and the bus lumbers over the Coast Range. Several miles south of the mouth of the river, the bus turns right and heads up the Pacific coast. I imagine the ocean just a few feet away. I feel a sense of floating north as the waves caress the edge of the highway, sometimes leaping inland and lapping the wheels of the bus.

Coyote watches me. He knows the shape of my eyes as I slip into a daydream.

"Just wait," says Coyote. "You ain't seen nothing yet!"

Hours later, hungry, dog-tired, ears numb from the whine of the bus engine and noses and throats stinging with diesel fumes, we arrive at Siletz.

At first, the place seems empty. There are no cars in the parking lot. The tribal center is locked. I bang on the door. No answer. No one is around. We wander down the hill and find crowds of folks walking toward the dance house.

Inside, a hundred people crowd onto benches to listen to Coyote's grandmother tell an ancient story. In firelight, native-brown eyes gleam like the eyes of the ancestors. The fire blazes. The smell of smoke lives in the cedar planks. Coyote and I settle into the audience, and the weariness of the long bus trip is soon forgotten.

Grandmother Coyote puts on the mask of the creator and balances the mood of the place: the maleness of the fire, the traditional memory of the femaleness of the house—owned and run by women for longer than any man might want to remember—the female face behind the male mask, the womanly grace of movement and nurturing words as she describes the journey of Hapkemnas through the world he has created.

"First I dig into Mother Landscape, into the rich soil of the earth. This releases the myths. Now every home will be filled with stories. Then I put a post at each corner of the house pit, connect them with rafters, and balance a ridge pole over the top."

Her story of Hapkemnas travels the night along the length of the river, from Daldal's house at the mouth to the dwelling places of Old Time spirits at Boundary Springs. Each house along the river's path has a story, and the people who live there are eager to share. At the first glimmer of morning light, as the fire glows in its bed of orange coals, she removes the mask. Her face and the mask have the same deep creases as if they share the hills and valleys of the landscape. Perhaps they were both present at creation. No native storyteller who knows Old Time myths would argue which was older: Hapkemnas stories or Coyote stories. The fashioning of the homeland and the trickster-inspired reshaping of that landscape have common beginnings and speak as strongly to native people today as they did to their ancestors centuries ago.

"You have heard enough of this story. Too many words and your ears will grow long from too much listening. Now it's time for you people who come from the creator to go out and greet the morning and live in the wide world. Gweldi. Baybit leplap. This story is finished."

Grandmother Coyote notices Coyote and me at the back of the lodge. She glances toward the door and whispers to herself, "It's time to go on a journey."

The three of us walk. Before Mythtime, what is here is the land. Like a camera lens focusing on the main image for a film, Mother Landscape comes into focus. Each hill, each rock, each bend in each river has a story that is told in sight and sound, in the reddish blush of the first sunrise and the silver rising of the first moon, the flash of each star blinking on, the gurgling of springs in the mountains, the swish and swoosh of rapids and riffles, the stretching sound of roots as they push the first plants and trees into meadows along rivers and creeks. On this morning, a breeze rattles spring leaves. Fields are lush with new grass, tinted blue with blooming camas. Before Human People, before the Dragonfly brothers, before Hapkemnas, many of the Old Time stories are already here. Mother Landscape, the oldest storyteller, is always ready for an audience who is willing to watch and to listen.

As we walk through the film of our story, history looms in the fuzzy background and around the blurred edges. We get glimpses of fences and ranches, villages and towns, wagon roads and highways, people arriving and people leaving. Each night, in the light of our campfire, the background and edges of the film crowd closer into the center of what is seen and heard, images shapeshifting, stepping through shadows, in and out of flickering firelight, sounds of stories as words arrive one by one and join themselves into narratives. There are moments when the stories of this place, in all their wonder and their terror, become complete, when each image is fully in focus, when all of the characters have arrived and are ready to speak.

As we crest a hill and turn inland, I look back for a last glimpse of the ocean.

At the mouth of the Siletz River I see islands in the bay, stumps and logs carved by harsh coastal weather. From this distance, the islands rise through fog and hauntingly resemble Old Time Indian burials. I see the thousands of native people, shipped and force-marched hundreds of miles to a skeletal cluster of shacks and shelters that is the Siletz Indian Reservation of 1856. Government troops execute those who refuse to leave their homeland. They are shot in front of friends and relations to graphically illustrate that the US Government is serious about relocating natives.

Leaving their homes of thousands of years behind them, with only a basket of food each and the clothes on their backs, the trip to the reservation is long and sad. Captain Ord writes in his journal: "It almost makes me shed tears to listen to their wailing as they totter along." Many die along the way of various diseases, and many more die during the first winter from starvation, exposure, and sadness.

Housing is nearly nonexistent. New arrivals are sick from food unsuited to their usual diets. Many are fed flour normally sold as cattle feed, swept from the floors of Willamette Valley mills. Nightly bed checks keep track of who is where. Forts are built along the boundaries to prevent escapes. Family members are located in different areas. Indeed, early reservation life resembles life in a prison rather than in a community. Within a few years, an alarming number of native people will die from a depression of spirits. Ten years later, the dying will hardly slow. In the words of a Shasta elder, "Many of my people have died since they came here. Many are still dying. There will soon be none left of us. We are sick at heart. We are sad when we look on the graves of our families."

On this morning, the coastal weather continues shaping the islands at the mouth of the river. I step through fog and walk along the beach. Just offshore, I hear a mixture of shouting and crying. I see the ghostly outline of an old steamship heading north. I squint and make out the name on the side: Columbia. The morning is cold. The ship is crowded with native people being hauled to the reservation. I hear soldiers singing: "Columbia's sons and adopted daughters shriek aloud o'er land and waters. The Indians have come to quarters."

I shake my head and try to free myself from the vision. I turn and see Grandmother Coyote watching me. "I know where you've been," she says. The three of us walk in silence into the town of Dayton. We pass the old Fort Yamhill blockhouse and jail. Dark eyes stare out through the bars and follow our every step. We walk out of town, south through the Willamette Valley, toward home.

At the end of a long day, we arrive at Coyote Creek Crossing. A few inches below the surface is a rock shelf that inspired its earlier name of Rock Creek. This made for an easy bit of wading back in the old days and handy for wagons traveling the Old Trail. In 1856, the Trail of Tears crossed here. A Takelma woman is buried under the limbs of an age-old oak, one of several deaths along this trail. In the purple twilight, voices drift our way. We walk down the creek to have a look.

The path opens into a large meadow. We stand in the shadows just beyond a ring of light that comes from a campfire where Coyote Creek flows into the Long Tom River. What Coyote and I see next is an eye-opener. There we are, both of us, sitting around that fire with the oldest man I have ever seen. I blink my eyes and he disappears.

"This is nothing," whispers Grandmother Coyote. "Keep watching."

The moon clears a ridge and moonlight brightens the meadow. We watch in amazement as the shadows of the three of us slip away and sneak into the firelight.

This is the first time I have actually seen the Shadow People. Each morning I call for my shadow to come home after he's been out for the night visiting friends. Now there is a trio of Shadow People, mine among them, and I watch as if I am witnessing an old story that makes mythic images dance in my mind. Coyote's shadow splits in half, and now there are two of them.

My shadow stands next to Grandmother Coyote's shadow, and we watch her two grandsons tell a story together. After arguments about which of them is the one true Coyote-hero of the myths, followed by a tail-pulling tussle, they settle into the narrative, content that the contrived substance of their version of the story will make them both look good.

They improve on the world the creator made, they trick a village of pudgy, self-serving Frog People and bring water to this vast meadow that will come to be known as Grand Prairie. It is a magical myth. The moon disappears into the clouds. The fire burns down, no longer providing a spotlight for the happy, vainglorious tellers. The story is done and our shadows return.

I feel whole. It's not just having my shadow home that brings this feeling of fulfillment. There's something about hearing a story in this place. Despite its Coyote-stilted telling, it fills the landscape in an authentic way. For a moment, this native world seems balanced and I feel like I fully belong here. The last words of the story echo in my head: "That's just how it happened a long time ago."

We walk back down the creek and camp at the crossing, throwing our bed rolls under the oak tree. Grandmother Coyote sits by the grave and sings to the night, "Let us dream of our ancestors. May their stories be with us as we journey home."

The next day we traipse through history and myth, newsreels and old photos in and out of focus as we walk out of the Willamette Valley and into the mountains. We pass a carved boulder that maps the pattern of local creeks and rivers. Grandmother Coyote tells me that an important Kalapuya man is buried under that rock. "A sacred place," she says. "Some say that the Rock People are his ancestors." We rest at Grave Creek Crossing. Another grave, another song, another prayer. We journey south, deeper into spring. Blossoming fruit trees, hillsides purple with vetch, the people on the move … new beginnings after long winter nights. We follow our path as it climbs the slopes of Sexton Mountain.

As we crest the summit, we arrive at what appears to be a typical log home of the 1850s. But as we open the door and walk inside, we might just as well have stepped into a traditional plank house. The first home built by Hapkemnas would have looked much the same: dirt floor pounded smooth, mat-covered ledges for sitting and sleeping, and a fire in the center sending smoke in spirals through an opening in the roof. The fire is the only light, and it takes a few moments for me to notice an old woman sitting in the shadows. Her face looks as serious as stone, yet she is up in an instant, greeting Grandmother Coyote as if they were old friends. Her friendly gesture draws us farther inside.

Coyote elbows me. "Listen carefully to this one," he says. "She's never been one for chitchat. All of her news hides inside her story."

We all sit around the fire and the old woman starts her tale.

Rock Old Woman used to live here. The rock that looks like her is still out back. In the old days there were visitors every night. Those walking the path stopped by to leave an offering on the rock and thank her for their good health. Then the one who kept this house offered them a place to sleep, good food and good stories, and sent them on their way in the morning, their baskets fuller than when they arrived. Few folks stop by these days except for you people and one wanderer a while back.

He was a strange fellow. His hood covered most of his face. It was hard to see his eyes. He spoke with the voice of one who has been places.

"I have seen them," he said. "Canoes filled with ghosts, all heading downriver toward the Land of the Dead."

That's all I could get out of him. I couldn't tell if he was remembering the myth about Coyote killing the ghosts or had just seen the people forced from their homes. Or maybe something about the Ghost Dance. That night I did the talking until we both started dozing. In the morning, he was gone when I woke up. But he left behind a slip of paper with some writing on it. I guess that was his way of sharing his story. I remember the words …

"I fell sleep beside the river and dreamed of the Dark Woman. She walked lightly across a meadow. The crickets stopped singing. The woman stopped under a tree by the river and whispered a prayer. A gentle rain began to fall and woke me up, and she was gone. I caught a glimpse of her shadow as she walked upriver."

That's the end of her story. We stretch out on the mats, and the old woman stokes the fire. My sleep is sound and dreamless. In the morning we say goodbye and thank her for her kindness. At midday we reach the Rogue River and begin the last part of our walk, upriver toward the village of Ti'lomikh.

"Well, Mister Storyteller," says Coyote. "We're almost home. Have you been following this narrative? Have you been scribbling notes?"

"I lost the sequence," I say. "Time seems a little confusing, kind of chopped up."

"Welcome to how old stuff has become what it is now."

"Oh, you Coyote guy," says Grandmother Coyote. "Always chasing your own words."

"That's how it's always been," says Coyote. "We'll soon be home where we started, but not quite."

I stretch my legs to get ahead, out of earshot. I stride upriver through the town of Gold Hill. It is evening when I cross the river and walk into the village. I stand by myself for a few moments. Then stories arrive and the village gets crowded.

◇◇◇◇◇

Fog rolls into the village and smells of smoke. I walk past a smoldering house. The ridge pole has fallen, and the house collapsed into its own pit. I hear shouting. A horse pulls a plow across a cleared field. With each clink of the plow's blade, an old burial is exposed. Shouts erupt from a crowd of people. Each one paid an admission fee to watch the Indian graves get dug up. A young man bends down in the field. He is wearing a broad-brimmed hat and has a pipe in his mouth. He uses a trowel to dig. He removes bones and artifacts: an obsidian blade, shells, pine seeds, a bone ornament. The man scribbles in his notebook: "All undisturbed skeletons were lying on the left side with the head toward the south, facing west."

Downriver, I'm thinking. Downriver toward the Land of the Dead.

I walk deeper into the village past the last house, out of the fog and the smoke and into a large meadow. Coyote and his grandmother have somehow gotten ahead of me. They stand next to a yellow dome tent. A man sits on the grass, laptop on his knees, talking with Grandmother Coyote and typing away.

I walk up and Coyote whispers to me, "He's a writer and he just got here. Now Grandmother is telling him about this place, and he's adding it to his own story."

I gaze out across the river. The falls are wild with snowmelt. I imagine sitting on the rock above the falls. Loud, powerful, ancient. I turn back and Grandmother Coyote and the man have disappeared.

"Where did they go?" I ask.

"That writer fellow crawled into his tent."

"What about your grandmother?"

"I'm not sure," says Coyote. "Downriver somewhere. There were a lot of people walking toward the canoe landing. They were drumming and singing. I think she went with them."

Coyote and I stand on the riverbank. Two bright blue dragonflies lift off a rock and fly across the water and disappear. The Rogue River flows toward the last bit of sunset. Ti'lomikh waits for a new day.

THE YELLOWJACKETS STEAL
COYOTE'S SALMON

Along the Shasta River, the people tell this story.

There were many people living along the river near Mount Shasta. They had built a fish weir across the river and were busy catching and drying salmon.

A ways upriver, toward the mountain, Coyote was feeling hungry (which is how he felt most of the time) and feeling lazy (which is how he felt most ALL of the time). But instead of going out and getting his own food, he decided to travel downriver and mooch some dried salmon.

Those people saw Coyote coming a long ways off, and they were saying, "Oh, oh, here comes Coyote, that master mooch and trouble maker. Hide your riches, hide your food, keep an eye on your wives and daughters. Brace yourselves, here he comes!"

Coyote walked up and said, "Hello, friends. How about giving a weary traveler some of that salmon to get him back home?"

"So who's this person you're talking about?"

"Why, me, of course. I've been working for days trying to find food, but good stuff like this salmon never comes my way."

The people gathered together and talked it over. "I don't know," said one man. "We work hard for this salmon, and Coyote never works for anything, let alone hard work. I say we tell him to go get his own food. 'Weary traveler,' that's a laugh." Another man said, "Maybe so, but it never was good manners to send a traveler on his way without food when he asks for it. And if that's all Coyote wants, I say let him have it. There are some things harder to give up than salmon. Think of your daughters." The people talked a bit longer and decided to give Coyote some salmon to keep him from doing something drastic, hoping he'd just go away and leave them alone. They gave him a huge pile of salmon and sent him on his way.

Coyote packed it all on his back and went traveling back upriver, toward his home near Mount Shasta, grinning to himself as he went along. He hadn't gone far before that heavy pack of salmon tired him out. So he stretched out in the shade along the river and started snoring into a deep sleep, the pack of salmon under his head for a pillow.

There had been some yellowjackets following him upriver, their eyes and their taste buds focused on that fine catch of salmon Coyote was carrying on his back. They came swarming around Coyote while he slept, swarmed close to get a good look at the salmon under Coyote's head.

One of them said, "Serves the idiot right. He's always pulling tricks on people." Another said, "Now how are we going to get the stuff from under his head without waking him up?" "No problem," said a third yellowjacket. "Once the lazy sap is asleep, nothing short of the mountain blowing to smithereens will rouse him, and only then if he's hungry." "Okay, now," said the first yellowjacket, "let's all work together. Everyone call in brothers and sisters and cousins. This is going to take everyone we can muster."

Before long there were so many yellowjackets swarming over Coyote that it looked like a huge cloud of yellow smoke had balanced on his nose. But still he slept, snoring and snoring.

Now they went to work. Some of the yellowjackets lifted Coyote's head, and some of them lifted the pack of salmon, and others replaced it with a pack of pine bark. Then they all helped carry the salmon away—that pack looking like it was floating—upriver toward Mount Shasta. And they were laughing the whole way, which is quite a funny sound, an entire cloud of yellowjackets all giggling and belly-laughing at once.

Coyote started yawning, one eye half open, the other still closed, and his mouth, anticipating the salmon, going num-num-num, drooling a little over his chin. He turned over, still half asleep, took a bite out of his pillow only to find not salmon, but pine bark and slivers running every which way into his tongue.

Coyote jumped to his feet. "What's going on here? I'm the trickster in these parts. Nobody's going to steal my reputation. I'll find whoever did this and fix him good."

Coyote started sniffing circles around the place he'd slept, searching for tracks. "Now that's funny," he was thinking. "No tracks. Pretty tricky one, this fellow."

So Coyote, having no clues and hungrier than ever—even with his tongue speared full of slivers, which didn't seem to curb his tongue or his hunger—started back downriver to where the people were drying salmon.

It didn't take long for word to get out. "Coyote is coming downriver again," people were saying. "And he looks pretty mad." People were hiding their valuables when Coyote came stomping into their camp. His ears were steaming. "I need more salmon!" he demanded. "Some monster came while I was sleeping and stole all the salmon you gave me."

All the people went, "Whew! So that's all he wants."

They gave Coyote a heap of salmon and a place to sleep the night well away from where everyone else slept, and in the morning they sent him on his way.

Coyote went on, and he started puffing at the same place he got tired before, just a little ways upriver from where the people were drying salmon. Again he stretched out in the shade along the riverbank, and again he put the salmon pack under his head for a pillow. But he had only pretended to be tired—he'd stuck his tongue out and made it limp—and he only pretended to go to sleep, yawning at just the right time, slowly pulling his eyes closed. He was dramatically convincing. And sure enough, the yellowjackets had been following him, keeping their eyes on that salmon.

They called in all their relations and came swarming down on Coyote. Coyote was watching and thinking, "It can't be them. Yellowjackets always land on salmon." But the yellowjackets swarmed down on the salmon and groaned and moaned and moved it a bit. Coyote was watching. The yellowjackets tugged and tugged, and they lifted the pack, and they took off with the salmon, upriver toward Mount Shasta.

Coyote jumped up and took off after them, but he only got a little ways before he pooped out. He rested a while, watching his salmon float away in the distance, listening to those yellowjackets whoop and laugh, then he went back downriver to where people were drying salmon.

The people saw him coming, and they said, "Oh, no! Here he comes again!" Everyone braced themselves for Coyote as he came stomping into the camp. "You won't believe it!" Coyote yelled. "A huge cloud of a monster came right out of the sky and stole my salmon. It carried all that salmon through the air toward the mountain, laughing a crazy laugh the whole way." It didn't take long before Coyote's story spread all through the camp and a large crowd of people gathered around Coyote, asking him all kinds of questions and patting him on the back for being brave enough to run after the monster. "It was nothing," grinned Coyote. "Nothing at all. I do this sort of thing all the time."

The people gave him more salmon. He packed it on his back and traveled upriver, a great crowd of folks following behind hoping to get a chance to see the laughing yellow monster.

◇◇◇◇◇

Coyote stopped to rest at the same place, and the people gathered all around, hiding behind bushes and trees and rocks, all through the woods along the river.

A while later, Turtle came up and joined the crowd, and Coyote saw him and laughed, "Hey, you little runt, who asked you to come here, you little hard-backed, pin-eyed runt? What do you think you can do, you puny thing?"

Turtle didn't say a word. He only hissed a little at Coyote and sat by the river, apart from the others, looking like a river rock.

Now the yellowjackets came swarming in. Coyote quickly pretended to be asleep, the salmon pack for a pillow, and in the same way, the yellowjackets ripped off Coyote's salmon, grunting and wheezing as they were lifting, then laughing all the way upriver, flying toward Mount Shasta.

The people all came out from their hiding places and started running upriver after the yellowjackets, a long line of people racing up the river valley toward Mount Shasta.

Coyote was the first one to drop out, exhausted and droop-tongued. One by one others dropped out, and they made a long line of exhaustion along the river. But Turtle, who had started last, kept plugging along, and as he passed Coyote he hissed, "I haven't even started running yet."

Turtle went on and on, passing everyone, all the way up Mount Shasta, following the yellowjackets up the slopes of the mountain until they disappeared into a hole at the peak, salmon and all.

One by one, the people rested up—Coyote included—and they puffed and they puffed and they puffed their way clear to the top of Mount Shasta, where Turtle was waiting at the hole the yellowjackets had gone down.

When Coyote arrived, he took charge. "Let's smoke that monster out of its hole. Come on, everyone, gather some wood. Let's get on with it."

All the people went down the slopes, gathered wood, and brought it back to Coyote, who piled the wood in a heap in front of the hole and lit it.

Coyote fanned the smoke into the hole with his tail. Turtle was looking downriver, and he said, "Looks like your smoke is coming out down the valley a ways."

Coyote scrambled down the mountain, plugged the hole the smoke was coming out, then rushed back up and fanned more smoke into the original hole.

Now Turtle said, "Hey, Coyote, your smoke is coming out around the bend there."

So Coyote ran and plugged up THAT hole and came back around, fanning and puffing, fanning and puffing.

Turtle said, "Now it looks like the smoke is coming out a hundred holes all over the mountain and all down the valley."

Coyote went crazy plugging holes, but every time he stopped one up, another one started puffing smoke. Finally, Coyote went down the mountain, muttering, "Rabbits. Maybe that yellow monster doesn't like rabbits. Anybody got any rabbits?"

The people went back down the mountain, Turtle following behind making his own pace, and they got back to work drying salmon, shaking their heads and chalking up another misadventure to Coyote.

On the top of Mount Shasta, deep in their hole, the yellowjackets laughed as they ate, convinced that smoked salmon was more tasty than dried salmon.

And the mountain puffed smoke for a long, long time.

NIGHT OF GHOSTS, NIGHT OF STORIES

On a late night in October, a bright moon peers down on Dragonfly Place, where Coyote and I live in the Siskiyou Mountains. Deer move out of the trees and browse across a mountain meadow turned white by moonlight. Two owls call to each other from the depths of the woods. In the deep silence of the night, I am startled awake by unsettling images that linger from a dream. I wake up with the thought that a story awaits me down the valley at Rock Point, and I need to go have a look.

I shake Coyote awake. "Want to go for a ride?"

"Nice try, Doty. That only works on the lesser breeds."

"Ah, come on. I thought coyotes were somewhat nocturnal. Doesn't any coyote worth his gophers yearn to be out in the thick of things? Aren't you curious?"

"Nope. You must be thinking of those poor workhorse pooches who have to sweat for a meal."

"But there's a story waiting for us, and you're in it, and there is a creepy cemetery with fog. And ghosts! You don't want to miss yet another chance at mythic immortality, do you?"

"Now you're talking my lingo, Mister Storyteller. Make me a cozy bed in your rig, and I'll come along."

In an unexpected leap of energy, Coyote is out the door and down the steps before I can think of a satisfactory reply. I hear Coyote outside.

"Hi-yo, Doty's rig! Away!"

In the white light of the moon, Coyote and I drive down the mountain ridge. On modern roads, we follow the old stagecoach route through Jacksonville and around the fringe of the Rogue Valley. Moonlight is everywhere: on the peak of Mount McLoughlin, slanting across the flat tops of the Table Rocks. As we cross the Rogue River, moonlight sparkles on riffles and rapids.

I park my rig in the parking lot near the old hotel, which is now a tasting room for the vineyards. Behind the hotel and from the edge of nearby Rock Point Cemetery, rows of grapevines climb the hillside. A few cars speed down the road and disappear into darkness. The moon hangs over the night.

As I wait for some interesting story to arrive and reveal itself, Coyote gets bored and curls into doggy sleep. An hour creeps by. My eyelids grow heavy, and I begin to drift into a dream of a story. An old picture of this place from the late 1800s forms in my mind, and Coyote and I wander into that picture.

I am a self-appointed Old West wordsmith. Me and my legendary sidekick, Cowpoke Coyote, arrive by stagecoach at the Rock Point Hotel and Stage Station. It is Halloween night along the Rogue River. Among trees and tombstones, a green fog forms in the cemetery, creeps across the moon-white field toward the river, and mixes with dust kicked up by the stage as it rattles to a stop. Coyote and I walk through fog toward the hotel and into a spooky night of stories.

The hotel is a classic stage station, a two-story white building with a balcony that juts out from its second-floor ballroom. A white fence surrounds the yard, and firs and pines spread speckled shadows of their limbs across the roof and walls. Guest rooms are upstairs, and downstairs are parlors and a kitchen. On this night, the stage station shines ghostly white in the moonlight.

Cowpoke Coyote's ears poke through his cowboy hat. "Nothing I like better than poking cows," smirks Coyote. He says this to me as he pulls his hat off his ears, and we walk inside.

"Are you a cowboy or a coyote man?" I ask.

"Both," says Coyote. "And more! I'm Every Coyote. I'm older than any cowboy around here and as wise as any old man soon to be a ghost. I'm as young in spirit as any boy, and I can herd entire landscapes of cows with a single howl." Coyote stops dead in his tracks. "Wait a minute, what's that?"

Coyote notices a young boy and his black, one-eyed cocker spaniel. The two pooches eye each other cautiously, but their stares soften as they sense a familiar camaraderie. The hounds curl into snoozing postures on opposite ends of the stone hearth, near the blaze of the fire. I watch the boy and remember my youth and the hours I spent sitting in firelight listening to stories.

Gwisgwashan, a native elder, walks slowly down the stairs from her room. In shifting shadows and flickering firelight, she looks ancient, her face wrinkled and creased. She is the Keeper of Stories. Her people have lived here for a long time.

Gwisgwashan leans toward the boy. "Well, Tommy. Do you think that this is a good night for stories?" The boy nods with youthful enthusiasm. His dog, Tippy, dusts the hearth with her tail.

A short woman smelling of lilacs comes in from the kitchen, carrying steaming cider and mulled wine on a tray. "Something to warm your bellies on a chilly night?" She leaves the drinks and disappears into the back of the hotel.

I glance through the window into moonlight. I see a man walking across the field toward the hotel. He wears a hooded cloak and carries a lantern that sways from side to side with each step. As he walks through the fog, the hooded man vanishes and reappears, and the lantern glows green. The man approaches the hotel, opens the door, and enters. He sets his lantern on the mantel and keeps his cloak on as he settles into a chair near the fire. The hood flops over his forehead and hides his eyes.

Gwisgwashan turns his way. "Mr. Lampman. Welcome. Good to see you. I was about to tell Tommy an Old Time story." Lampman raises his arm in a gesture that encourages Gwisgwashan to tell her tale.

Gwisgwashan sits on a short stool in front of the fire. She is a silhouette, her face hidden in darkness as though the words were all that mattered in her story. But suddenly she turns, and the light catches her face sideways. Her eyes shine, and with the sweep of an arm gesturing the start of a story, she begins.

The old stories tell us that spirits wandered this place long before the cemetery or this hotel were here. This stretch of river has always been a gathering place for stories. Some stories dramatize our hopes, others give life to our fears. Some drift in and out as ghosts, some mingle with the fog and move along the river. Some of the stories are older than anyone can remember.

Along the Rogue River here at Rock Point, this place we call Titankh, on a night when the oak trees were wintertime bare and the water cold and the air green with fog, Coyote was creeping along, looking for a meal: creep … creep … creep … creep … creep …

From out of the fog, Coyote heard voices. "Ghosts are taking away people." That's all he heard. "Ghosts are taking away people."

Coyote stopped. "What does it mean when people say that? I'd better go downriver and find out. When people die, they are not supposed to take others with them, yet now I hear people saying, 'Ghosts are taking away people.' I'd better find out why they are saying such things."

Coyote walked downriver along the ghost trail toward the Land of the Dead: creep … creep … creep … creep … creep …

Moonlight cast a narrow trail of light upon the river, pointing the way. Along the riverbank, shadows of trees seemed to move as Coyote and the ghosts moved. As Coyote went along, ghosts walked beside him: chirp … chirp … chirp … chirp … chirp …

Coyote picked up a pine cone and threw it toward the sound of the ghosts and kept on walking, following the ghost trail: creep … creep … creep … creep … creep …

He walked on and on, downriver into thicker fog, into deep cold, into darker forests. He arrived at a meadow across the river from the Land of the Dead. He heard ghosts talking on the other side.

"Look! Coyote has come here. Someone take him a canoe so he can come across. Let's invite him to visit his death."

Coyote squinted. Through the fog he saw the dim shapes of the ghosts. They were dancing a young woman dance. They wore the clothes they had been buried in, hanging in strips and tatters. They were dancing: chirp … chirp … chirp … chirp … chirp …

Now Coyote sat on the edge of the river and built a fire. As he was smoking his pipe, a young girl brought him a canoe. She waded toward the bank, through the fog and the cold water, holding onto the canoe.

"Come on up here on the land, child," said Coyote. "That water is cold. Come up here and share my fire."

"Oh, no, Coyote. I know your tricks. You come down here and I'll take you across. Aren't you curious?"

"Now why would I want to go over there? Come to the riverbank, child."

"No, Coyote. Quick, come to the canoe and I'll paddle you across."

Coyote got mad. "Come to the land!"

The young girl came up on the bank and stood next to Coyote.

"Quick, Coyote, let me take you across."

Coyote reached to the fire and grabbed a flaming stick off the top. It looked like he was about to light his pipe again, but in a sudden movement, he turned and lit the girl's skirt on fire.

That girl was a ghost and she started burning: doo … doo … doo … doo … doo … She ran to the water, got in her canoe, and paddled across the river. The canoe blazed as it crossed the river to the Land of the Dead.

The ghosts were still dancing: chirp … chirp … chirp … chirp … chirp …

The young girl ran in among them and started dancing, and her burning skirt set fire to all of the dancers. Now they were burning. The ghosts were blazing in one big circle dance of fire: doo … doo … doo … doo … doo …

Late in the night, the flames died down and the fire smoldered, its pale smoke mingling with the fog.

Coyote called out, "Now you are dead! You will no longer take people with you when you die. In later times, your place will be a place of sunshine. People will come here and live happy lives after they have died. But they will not bring living people with them!"

In the first light of morning, Coyote walked back upriver toward his home, looking for food: creep … creep … creep … creep … creep … The sun sparkled on the river. Flowers started blooming. The river rushed along through the first warm air of spring.

The ghosts had been killed.

Before anyone says a word, Lampman pulls back his hood. His eyes flare wild in the flickering light. He speaks with a voice that is deliberate, as if the words come not from himself, but from deep inside his story.

"Perhaps Coyote burned those Old Time ghosts, but he didn't burn them all. Others have arrived since then, and more are yet to come. Some are with us now. I walk among trees, between graves, along the river, and I have seen things.

"My tale takes place a few years after the white man's war on the native people of this land. The Takelmas had been force-marched from here to the coast, and those who didn't die of sadness along the way were locked up on the reservation. But a few stayed behind in their homeland, hiding out in the mountains and here along the river.

"There was a night when the cemetery stretched and reached deep into the woods, its craggy fingers grabbing at the green fog of the ancient forest. I had been told by an Indian friend of mine that this green fog was the spirit of the Tree People reaching out to claim the homeland that once was theirs … now cleared fields, stage roads, towns.

"I walked through fog upriver to one of the old village sites. In the last glimmer of twilight, I heard drumming and singing. As I walked closer, I saw a campfire, and in that light five dancers circled a giant pine that had been girdled partway up, its bark removed. The pine tree rose from a jumble of cairns, all that remained of the village graveyard. The dancers sang the songs of their ancestors, dancing their ghosts to life, coaxing them out of their graves with familiar songs.

"I moved in closer, and listened and watched. The dance rebuilt the village. Plank houses and sweat lodges rose from the soil, several dance rings emerged, and many fires flared through the night.

"The faces of the dead wore masks. They moved among the living, transparent in the firelight. Some were animals, some human, and a few wore the expressions of the sun and moon. I saw the faces of the White Duck Women, Panther and Wildcat, Salmon Boy, Rock Old Woman. They were joined by others until generations of this village danced together. Some ghosts traveled far from their lives in the myths. Others arrived from a few years back.

"Years before, ghost dances had been held to raise the native dead into a force of warriors and drive away those who had taken everything from them that had been sacred in their lives. But this dance was different. The people sang and danced to share this night in their ancient village. It was a dance of sadness and celebration. It was too late for anything else.

"The dance went on until the first sunlight sent the spirits back to their graves and to their lives beyond the dead. The village collapsed into a jumble of cairns.

"Perhaps this dance had some of the power of previous dances. It worked on me. I walked away from the village and never went back.

"Some ghosts still wander this land. Coyote didn't burn them all."

"Hey! I've got a ghost story," says Tommy. "May I tell it? Please? It's my turn, isn't it?"

Tippy and Coyote perk up when they hear the boy's voice, wagging their tails with encouragement. Lampman draws down his hood and sips his wine. I lean forward in my chair, watching Tommy closely. This boy seems familiar.

"Of course," says Gwisgwashan. "The more stories the better."

Tommy stands up and walks toward the fire. He leans against the mantel and tells his story in a whisper.

"Friends of ours built a ranch house along the river not far from here. When they got settled in, they had a house warming party. And a strange thing happened. I was at that party, so I know that this is a true story.

"Around midnight we gathered in the living room around the fire. We were admiring the large mantelpiece, and we listened to the story of how the wood had once been the central beam in the rafters of an old barn.

"As the clock chimed twelve, we heard a loud creak creak creak coming from the mantelpiece. There were also sounds of choking and horses whinnying and stomping and hoof beats like someone quickly riding away.

"The owners of the house asked around and found that on that night, years before, a gang of outlaws hanged a man at midnight from that same beam in the barn, and then they quickly fled their crime on horseback.

"Every year at midnight, on the anniversary of the hanging, the choking man is heard swinging from the rafters until he is dead. Creak creak creak …"

The fire crackles and collapses into coals. Lampman's lantern sputters and goes out. Hoof beats shatter the silence.

The short woman smelling of lilacs rushes into the room. "What's this? There's no stage expected tonight. Not this late. And why are they going so fast?"

She peers through the window. "No one is there. This is spooky."

Coyote and Tippy are up, ears erect, noses sniffing. Cowpoke Coyote has his hat on, ready to poke or punch whatever bovine specter might stampede through the door.

"Shhh," whispers Gwisgwashan. "Listen for the story."

There is the faint sound of a crying baby and voices mixing with the sounds of many others wailing. Scattered words leak through the din. They are speaking Takelma. The native people are being forced from their homes. Those who escape their tears long enough to speak mutter to each other, asking questions and getting no answers, as if no one knows their destination. One voice rises above the others, "Where are we going? Reservation? Land of the Dead?" Another voice shouts back, "Perhaps they are the same place!" They march downriver and into silence.

A train hoots and rumbles past the stage station, heading upriver. A man shouts after it, "You can take your idea of progress somewhere else. We don't want no trains stopping around here!" Doors slam one after another. Men shout as they load furniture and boxes of possessions into wagons that rumble out of Rock Point, heading upriver toward the town of Gold Hill, where the train has screeched to a stop.

There is silence and a feeling of emptiness, as if this room of the hotel has become a ghost town.

Outside, the green fog spreads thin. Some fog joins the river and flows beyond sight, some creeps back into the cemetery, swirling around trees and tombstones, drawn back to its origins by those who still linger here from the old days.

Lampman lights his lantern, opens the door into moonlight, and trudges across the field, disappearing into the fog. Gwisgwashan walks upstairs to her room, and soon after, Tommy and Tippy wander home. The short woman smelling of lilacs is nowhere to be seen. The fire sputters and dies.

As I open my eyes in my rig, the sun sends its first light across the river. I glance to the hotel and see a faint flicker of firelight through the window and what looks like the shape of the short woman roaming from room to room. The morning smells like lilacs. I drift back to sleep.

A few hours later, a whisper from the back seat startles me fully awake.

"Chirp … chirp … chirp …"

"Stop it! You scared the living daylights out of me!"

"Not all the ghouls are dead, Mister Storyteller. Did you notice how that boy Tommy looks a lot like you? You might have been his ghost!"

"Wait a minute, how do you know about him? I thought that was my dream."

"You silly human with such small visions of what is possible. You don't know the old saying?"

"Yes?"

"Stories are dreams gone public. And I've seen them all."

"Right," I say. "Let's head home to Dragonfly Place. I need to write out this story."

"You mean write off those silly fears you humans have?"

"We worders don't write things off. We write them down."

"Right," says Coyote. "Let's go home. You can write and scare yourself with your ghost stories. Just don't forget I'm the main pooch in this tale. You can leave out that black one-eyed doggy. Remember, you promised me mythic immortality."

"Right. I'll scribble and you eat breakfast."

"Hi-yo, Doty's rig! Away!"

As we leave, the lights come on in the old hotel. An "Open" sign is hung on the fence, and cars pull into the parking lot. People walk across the porch and into the tasting room, where they sample wine.

I imagine this scene. The room fills with folks who have been traveling, and wine flows like the river. Near the fireplace, people share their stories like they have always done, here at this place where stories gather. Stories swirl through the day and into the evening. They revisit the stage station like ghosts. A few of the tales are older than anyone can remember.

As we cross the river, the sun sparkles on the surface. Oaks along the riverbanks are bright with their October colors of yellow and gold. The river rushes along through the first warm air of mid-morning.

DOG BRINGS FIRE TO THE PEOPLE

SITTING CLOSE TO THE FIRE, THE PEOPLE tell this story.

Back in the Old Time, after the great flood had put out all of the fires, nothing could be cooked. The people tried everything. They put their food out in the sun, but it spoiled. They soaked it in the hot springs, but it got soggy. Coyote tried cooking meat in his armpits, but he was the only one who liked how it tasted. Finally, the people gathered together and decided to send Owl to the top of Mount Shasta to have a look at the world and see if he could spot any trace of fire. That mountain was always puffing smoke. Fire had to be nearby.

Owl took a feather blanket with him and flew toward the mountain. Lizard watched him go. He could see far, and he told the people how Owl was getting on. A long while went by, and Owl didn't come back. The people thought he was dead. But Lizard said, "Quiet now, I can still see him."

At last Owl stood on the summit of Mount Shasta. He was tired, but he looked all around. He looked twice to the west and saw smoke coming from Fire Woman's house. He flew back to the village and said, "There is fire down there."

Next morning, the people got ready and went off west toward where Owl had seen the smoke. Everyone had a cedar-bark torch, and Dog had some dry tinder and punk hidden in his ear. They traveled all day, and late in the evening they arrived at Fire Woman's house. They asked to be allowed to warm their hands, and she invited them in.

Fire Woman's fire was crackling and blazing. Sparks jumped all around. Dog held his ear to the fire, caught a few sparks, and lit the tinder and punk. Everyone else thrust their torches into the fire and ran!

Fire Woman was angry, and she tried to hit them as they ran past her. They were a long line of runners now, critters and people, and everyone carried a flaming torch. They ran and they ran.

Back at her house, Fire Woman's fire began to die down. She sang a song and danced. She did a ceremony. She shouted, "Let the rain come." Bluejay heard her and screeched, "Qas!" and heavy rain poured down.

Coyote's torch went out first. Then another torch, and another. Dog held his head to one side to keep the rain out of his ear.

They ran as fast as they could. By the time they got back to their village, all the torches had gone out. The fires were gone except for that little bit that was burning inside Dog's ear.

The people were sad. No one had seen Dog bend his ear to the fire, and they thought fire was gone from them forever.

Dog started laughing. He danced round and round, howling, "I am sweating! I am sweating!"

That made Coyote angry. "Hit him! Knock him out! He laughs at us!"

Dog said, "Look in my ear."

When they lifted Dog's ear, they saw smoke and then fire. They took the tinder and punk and made a larger fire in one of the houses. Everyone came and gathered around the fire. They cooked a feast that tasted better than anything Coyote had ever made. And afterwards, they went outside and danced in the rain.

From that day on, Dog was the people's friend. They share their fire with him. He's part of their hearth.

WRITING ON THE ROCKS

Rock People are the oldest people. Their stories are told with symbols painted and carved on stone. The Takelmas call these stories se'l, or rock writings. One story tells how medicine people come to a rock in the mountains. They walk the crooked path to the top, where they have visions. When they return they have completed a sacred circle. Nearby is the home of Dan Mologol, a legendary healer from the Old Time and the first to walk the healing path. Her name means Rock Old Woman.

The rock writing symbol for completeness is a rope with the two ends tied together. Native people see their world in circles and cycles rather than straight lines. To tie the rope transforms it from a straight line to a circle, makes it complete. This symbol is frequently found at vision quest sites, a sacred place to journey to, experience days and nights of dreams and visions, and then return home. To native people, the message is clear: complete this journey to become a complete person.

Each time I visit my ancestral village of Coyote's Paw, I honor the long-time presence of the Rock People. They are everywhere. They gather over graves and make cairns, sit in circles around winter fires, circle dance the dance ring. All through the village they grind nuts and seeds. They cook acorn soup. They make a path for the creek. They heat the sweat lodge. Rock People line the trail to the Vision Peak, lingering in the shade of their old friends the Tree People. They are the first to greet me as I walk into the village and the last to say goodbye.

We paint and carve stories on stone where each story takes place. In villages, in caves, up and down rivers and creeks, out in the desert. These symbols help keep our stories alive. They give voices to the first storytellers, the oldest elders ... the Rock People.

I imagine this ancient scene.

Someone wrote a story on this rock, perhaps a thousand years ago, perhaps more. Someone who walked the woods at night. He went inside the cave, made a fire, and sat for a long, long time. He listened to the tumbling of the creek, to the slow growing of trees and the slower settling of the earth. Orange light from the fire danced across the rock.

He dipped his fingers in the paint he'd mixed. In strokes that matched the thickness of his fingers, he streaked symbols that told the story of this place ... the power of this cave.

Someone wrote a story on this rock, someone who had known the rock a long, long time.

Five years later the man brought his son to the cave and taught him how to mix the paint. In the light of the fire, the man explained the ideas behind the symbols and how they were arranged on the rock to tell a story. He explained that sometimes he carves the symbols into wood, sometimes into bone.

"When we've been out fishing all day," he told the boy, "we come home and play the hand game. But we've got to have a bone that looks different from the others. So we talk about the fishing, and as we're talking, I'm carving symbols into the bone. When we're done, we've got a record of what we did that day as well as a bone to play the game."

The boy asked him if he used the same system of symbols he used on the rocks.

"System?" the man replied. "No, not a system. Just the symbols we've always used."

The man and his son sat and listened to the creek and the trees and the earth. They watched the firelight bring the writings to life with symbols that told the story of this place so well. Then the boy dipped his fingers in the paint and, with shy, tentative strokes, began to add his own perceptions to the story.

FIVE NIGHTS
AT MEDICINE ROCK

SOMETIMES THE STORIES OF MY HOME FEEL foreign. I was born and raised in southern Oregon, where generations of my family lived before me. I travel widely, but the stories of my people always bring me home. I hear those stories as I walk the landscape, searching for a mythic encounter that is always around the next bend. There are deep layers of stories I have yet to experience, stories I thought I knew well. Until I find them, my heart beats a restless rhythm, and parts of the stories seem just out of reach. In some of those stories, I feel like a visitor.

The latest journey in my search begins in a museum in the small town of Talent. I'm with Coyote in the research library looking at maps.

"Look," I say. "Here's the Rogue River." I trace a route on the map with my finger. "The old Indian trail goes along here, and on this ridge, that's Medicine Rock. I've never been there."

Coyote's eyes twinkle and he chuckles. "You know where the rock is, don't you?"

Coyote leaps out of his chair and trots toward the door. "Need a guide?" he says with a smirk.

Before I can answer, he's out of the museum and heading for my rig. He leaps through the open window and lands in his doggy bed.

He howls, "Giddy-up, Doty's rig! Giddy-up!"

Half an hour later we are driving along a gravel road uphill from the river. Twilight surrounds us as we approach a locked gate blocking the road. There is just enough light to read the sign: "Rogue River Rock Quarry. No Trespassing. This Property Under Video Surveillance."

Medicine Rock is in a rock quarry? This biting irony is better than anything this storyteller could ever dream up.

"Yes," says Coyote, as if he could hear my thoughts. "We're headed into the rock-smashing place. Here's where we start walking." He lowers his voice to a whisper. "Just around that curve is the caretaker's cottage. He has a couple of guard dogs who like to snooze on the porch. We'd better tiptoe."

"Let me guess. We should let sleeping dogs lie?"

"Right you are. And I'm awake and I'm telling the truth."

"Not another wild dog chase?"

"Nope. These dogs are disturbingly domestic."

Coyote is a talker, and I have found it wise to allow him some slack in his linguistic leash when it comes to what he thinks is clever banter. Setting him up keeps him happy. But this is enough, and I walk on. As we creep past the cottage, the dogs stay stretched out on their sides, happy in their dreams. A full moon rises above the ridge, and the road ahead lights up. A couple of turns and we walk into the main part of the quarry. There is white rock everywhere. Moonlight is brilliant. Our shadows stretch across the landscape.

As I turn to say something to Coyote, I see him heading back down the road.

"Where are you going?"

"You need to do this by yourself. Here, take this. You'll need it!" He tosses a small stone my way and disappears into the shadows.

As I walk into the heart of the quarry, Coyote's stone feels comfortable in my hand, well-worn, a perfect fit. I stand and look around. The only rocks still intact—and the only trees—are high on the ridges. Between here and there are deep gouges in the earth where machines have removed the soil and found the rock layers underneath and then hammered them into gravel. There is white dust everywhere—on trucks and bulldozers, and on the metal tool shack. A cloud of dust hangs around the electric light above the door. My eyes scan the tops of the ridges until I spot a rock partially hidden by trees. The rock is tall and flat on top and stands by itself in the moonlight. That's got to be it, I'm thinking, and I start up the ridge.

It takes a while to get there. Loose gravel from the quarry work makes for chancy climbing, and I slide back a bit with each step. Handholds are few. But moonlight reveals the easiest way up, and eventually I find myself standing at the base of the rock.

The main rock leans toward another rock, creating a cave-like crevice between the two. I push my way through the scrub oak, side-stepping the poison oak, and walk inside. Even in the shadows I see the painted symbols, bright red on white rock. There is a series of images leading me into the cave, almost luring me to the back where there is a small hole that leads out. Some of the symbols are familiar. The long fingers that mean to look way up. Another symbol confirming that this is a good place hidden below. The squeezed lines indicating a narrow place. Footprints that show the path up and the return along a second path. A circle. A sacred journey to become complete. A moccasin print points the way. The exit in the back draws me forward.

I walk past the symbols, squeeze through the hole, and scramble up the ledge to the top of the rock. Here the world opens up. Despite the brilliance of the moon, stars are everywhere, wheeling and circling through the deep sky. I see ridge after ridge in the distance and the valley below, where the river winds toward the coast. I sit on a natural stone seat that faces east. Within reach is a pile of stones. I pull mine out of my pocket and add it to the pile. I glance back at the stars. This is the last thing I remember before I doze off and slip into the most dramatic dreams I have ever had … five nights of dreams as vivid as stories …

Here is my dream of the First People.

My old friend Rockman Jim appears in this dream. He's an old soul, a wanderer, and I haven't seen him in years. It's just like him to show up at this particular time and in a special place. He knows all about rocks. We meet on top of a cliff.

"I've been looking for the creator's cave for a long time," says Rockman Jim. "There's a symbol here that tells me this is the right place." He points to a weather-worn carving in the sandstone: a circle inside a circle, meaning a hollow place, a cave below. Before I can even get excited, Rockman Jim is halfway down the slope.

There is a fire near the entrance of the cave. As I walk in, I no longer feel inside my body. I am a shadow on the wall, a spirit outside of time, my movements controlled by flickering flames. Rockman Jim sits by the fire.

"Watch the rock wall for the Old Ones," he says. "They still come here to visit."

The fire flares and crackles as Rockman Jim tells me about the Rock People.

"They were the first people anywhere. Even before Hapkemnas the Children Maker made the world, the Rock People made this cave. When Hapkemnas was done with his work, he came here to live. The entrance looks down on his world. He watches the seasons spin through the year as the medicine people make their rounds. Each spring, Acorn Woman comes down from her craggy home on Mount McLoughlin to help the oak trees grow food for the people. Rock Old Woman walks from village to village keeping the people healthy, returning often to her home below the summit of Sexton Mountain. There are other mountain spirits, all spreading good medicine through the world. Each winter, Gwisgwashan, the Keeper of Stories, stops by and shares not only the old myths, but also the new ones that have been made since her last visit."

Rockman Jim tosses a log on the fire, and my shadow leaps deeper into the cave. I am not alone. There are other shadows, dozens of them, dancing on the cave wall.

"Here is a story. In the beginning, nothing. All was black. IT IS made a loud explosive sound and pointed at one spot. IT IS made white light and burst out of the darkness. A spirit circle of light, IT IS. From the center, a yellow flame giving out molten red earth."

My shadow whispers, "Who is IT IS?"

"IT IS was here when the Rock People arrived. There was always something around to make the world out of, you know. Maybe it's the ancestor of the earth herself. I know it's confusing. The old people used to say that Indians just grew, never came from anywhere."

Rockman Jim tosses water on the fire, and smoke smarts my eyes. When I open them, I'm the only one left in the cave. It's dark. I am back inside my body, and I can't see my shadow. I hear Rockman Jim singing somewhere outside.

"Rock People, Rock People, I cry. Dance my morning when I die."

I walk out of the cave and down into the valley, toward the Takelma village of Ti'lomikh.

◇◇◇◇◇

Here is my dream of the Human People.

The community house is large. It holds over a hundred people and sits near the edge of the river. From inside, even above the voice of the storyteller, I hear the wild rushing of the falls.

The storyteller is an old woman wearing worn leather clothing and a basket cap. She has the traditional woman's tattoo of three marks on her chin, and she leans on a staff carved with Animal People from her stories.

"We all know the story of Rock Boy," says the storyteller. "We have heard it around this fire many times on the long winter nights. We know about Rock Boy's birth, how he disappeared and Coyote found him. And we know all of the stories that come after. But few people know what happened to Rock Boy after this village was settled. I will tell you the rest of his story. He is still out there, wandering around."

The storyteller eases into a long story that I have trouble following, one I've never heard before, with words and phrases from some ancient version of the language. But clearly the native listeners know what's going on. They are tuned in to every word, every gesture, especially a young woman sitting in the back near the door. Her eyes are as wide as the river.

Here's what I do remember. The old woman's story is filled with ancient customs. If a rattlesnake bites your shadow, it is a sign that you will be sick. You must kill any black-striped snake that crosses your path. If you don't, one of your relatives will die. Beware of Bluejay imitating Eagle's screech. This is a sign of bad luck. Maybe someone will be killed with an arrow. And watch out for ghosts, the oldest spirits, especially on foggy nights. They are everywhere! They travel to and from the Land of the Dead along a strip of white cloud in the west. Sometimes they are seen as little lights at night along the old trails or heard as strange whistling noises in the trees: tsusum, tsusum, tsusum ... "Sometimes Rock Boy sounds just like that," says the storyteller.

She pauses. I hear that same sound from outside. At first I think it's the falls. But the young woman near the back hears it as well, and she stands up and opens the door. I follow her outside. The woman walks downriver past the cemetery. From down the trail, somewhere ahead of her, I hear the sound: tsusum, tsusum, tsusum ...

Behind me, I hear the falls crashing over rocks as well as the storyteller's voice as she continues her story.

The woman sings as she walks.

"Rock People, Rock People, I cry. Let the ghost be a dragonfly."

Here is my dream of the Medicine People.

This night is entirely its own. I walk behind the woman. Though there is no trail, she seems to know where she is going, up the ridge to the entrance of Medicine Rock. She walks inside. She places her hands on the smooth rock face. Her fingers trace the cracks as though they are exploring a map of the world or painting symbols with invisible paint. She walks through the crevice and finds her way to the top of the rock. She sings for the spirits of the old medicine people to come visit her.

She picks up a stone and looks at it closely. She sings a song to Rock Boy. She turns it over and sees a different shape and sings to Acorn Woman. More turnings ... Rock Old Woman, Mudcat Woman,

Medicine Fawn, all of the Old Time healers.

Between verses she strains to hear the sounds of the village: the falls, distant voices, someone drumming. She falls asleep, and inside her dream she hears herself singing. Days and nights go by as if time is defined by Dreamtime or Mythtime.

She leaves the stone on top as she makes her way down the slope. She walks around the outside of the rock to the entrance of the crevice. Five days later, she returns and paints the symbols of her ceremony on the inside walls. She completes the circle and starts a tradition. She is the first of many generations of medicine people to sit on top of the rock and dream about healing.

Here is my dream of the Quarry People.

This dream is a nightmare, loud, sharp, abrasive. I'm surprised I sleep through it!

Huge machines roar up the ridge. Mother Landscape shivers. Animal People escape into the woods. The machines go to work, clearing the forest, digging into the earth, scraping away the soil down to the rock. Creeks turn muddy with debris. Dirty water finds its way down the ridge to the river, pooling into brown clouds at the mouths of creeks. Dust makes the air thick and gritty. The sun is a blur.

As I watch the first rocks crushed into gravel and hauled away in trucks, I'm struck that this is another Trail of Tears. It's the same story happening again. The Rock People are being removed from their homeland, transported to new homes to live different lives. Some of their relations stay behind, hiding on the ridges, hiding in forests beyond the fringe of the quarry. They watch in silence as their age-old world is transformed. They hide out for decades.

The shift whistle blows. The machines shut down and everyone heads home, except for one fellow sitting in a dusty chair in front of the shack. I walk his way, and as I get closer I recognize Rockman Jim.

"Nice to see you," he says. "In case you're wondering what I'm doing here, let's just say that jumping from one dream to another is something we medicine folks do well."

"But here? You? What's up?"

"I'm the quarry manager. See? My own pickup, cell phone, a tin shack with a coffee pot—the works."

"You're kidding!"

"Nope. I'm needed here. New owners, you know, and they like the rock. Some scientist-types told them it's a sacred site, so the place has a new name: Medicine Rock Quarry. Like it?"

Before I can say something about cosmic irony, another whistle blows and I'm back on top of the rock.

Here is my dream of the Museum People.

I wake up inside another dream. I hear voices. People are working on the rock.

"Yikes! What's happening?" I'm thinking and say it out loud.

"The rock is moving," says Coyote.

"What are you doing here?"

"You look confused. I thought you might need an interpreter."

A power saw starts up and whines as it cuts through the rock, trimming the edges. The entire rock vibrates.

"Okay, Coyote, you want to tell me what's going on?"

"You're back in town. You're on a different rock—well, sort of. This one is a replica and is being sculpted out of concrete. I hired these rock artist guys. Good idea, huh? Hold on, they're going to carry it inside."

I look around. It's a sunny afternoon and I'm definitely in town. I duck as the rock is carried through the doorway of the museum and fitted into its new home near the entrance. I slide off the top and watch the workers from a distance. At the end of a long day, they pack their gear and head out. I stretch out on the floor and doze for a while.

It is nighttime when I open my eyes inside the museum. Moonlight shines through the window. I walk around the rock. I carefully paint the symbols as I remember them. Not knowing what else to do, I take out my grandfather's tobacco pouch, sprinkle tobacco over the rock, and recite a Takelma medicine poem. I turn to leave and see Coyote standing in the shadows, watching me.

"Nice looking fake rock," he says. "The Rock People might even like it."

"Was this your plan all along?"

"I don't make plans," says Coyote. "I just show up."

Coyote trots outside. I stand in front of the rock. I close my eyes and listen. I hear the footsteps of people walking an ancient trail, I hear the rushing of the river down the ridge, I hear singing drifting through the night. I can barely make out the words.

"Rock People, Rock People, I cry. My journey passes me by."

I turn and take a few steps toward home.

THE SNAKE

In many native cultures, Snake is a symbol of good luck and longevity. The Modocs believe that if Rattlesnake wraps himself around your leg and doesn't bite, you will live a long and lucky life. In a Coos myth, Snake and a young girl become friends, and Snake provides her village with food for generations. At the end of a storytelling, the teller says: "You've heard enough stories. If you listen to too many stories at one time, you'll have bad luck with rattlesnakes!"

Around fires on the beach, the people tell this story.

There was a girl who lived along a river where it flowed into the ocean. She lived with her five brothers and her parents. She swam every day, early in the morning, then again in the evening. She swam near the mouth of the river where she could watch the waves of the ocean crash onto the beach.

Early one morning, as she was swimming and the sun was just starting to come up, lighting the water until it almost glowed, she swam out to a deep pool in the river where it flowed slowly. She spotted a small snake swimming near the surface. The snake was so small that at first she thought it was a hair, but when she looked closely, she saw his eyes and the colors streaming down his back, bright in the morning sun.

The girl stretched out her hand, and the little snake swam onto it and coiled into a circle on her palm. The girl swam back to the shore carrying the snake on her hand and put him on a clump of moss while she dressed. Then she took the snake home with her.

She snuck him into the house so her parents and her brothers wouldn't see him. She snuck him to the corner where she slept. She gathered moss and made a bed next to her own bed, a fine little bed he could coil up on. The whole time the girl was thinking, "Such a strange little snake, I wonder what I'm going to do with him? And I wonder what he might do?"

The days went by. The snake grew bigger and bigger. His colored stripes shone brighter, all gold and blue. The girl swam every morning and every evening, and she always brought home fresh moss for the snake. She kept a close eye on him as he grew, and one morning, after coming home from swimming, she touched the top of his head and felt two lumps. The snake grew bigger every day, and the girl watched those lumps turn into horns.

Five years went by, and the girl became a young woman. The snake had grown so large that his horns stuck through holes in the roof of the house. He made so many coils as he lay next to the young woman's bed it was difficult to count them.

Her parents asked her, "What are you going to do with the snake?"

"I shall keep him and raise him," she answered.

One evening she was sitting on her bed, admiring the snake's coils and his brilliant colors, and she said to him, "I have no friends. Maybe you can be my friend. Maybe you can live here forever."

Next morning, the snake was gone.

The woman looked everywhere for him. "Where did he go?" she asked herself. She searched around the house and down by the river. She walked along the beach, looking and looking, then finally came back past the house and into the woods.

Deep in the woods she heard a great slithering sound. She saw the snake coming toward her, his giant horns and colors glowing, and he was carrying a deer in his mouth. He carried the deer to the house, then slithered back into the woods. By noon the snake had brought five deer and five elk to the house. Then he went inside, made giant coils by the woman's bed, and stuck his horns through the roof.

The woman and her brothers and parents worked hard skinning the deer and elk and preparing the meat. Before long the house was overflowing with food. The young woman was amazed at the snake—and a little frightened—but people were coming from other houses to trade for their extra food. That made her happy. Her family was getting rich.

Five days later the snake disappeared again. The young woman looked all over: in the woods, along the river, everywhere. The last place she went was to the beach.

She walked alone, looking out over the ocean, and she spotted a giant wave moving across. The young woman watched the wave grow bigger and bigger. As it came closer she saw the snake's horns rising over the water, then his eyes and his colored stripes, bright as the sun. When she looked closer, she saw he was carrying a whale in his mouth. The snake swam to the shore, left the whale on the beach, then swam back into the ocean. By noon he had left five whales on the beach, then he slithered back to the house.

While her family and neighbors were busy cutting up the whales, the young woman went inside her house. The snake was lying on his coils near her bed. She walked closer, and he spoke to her: "I cannot stay here. I am going home to the ocean. That is where I need to be. Whenever you see rough water you will know that I am nearby, and then I shall bring a whale to the beach for you and your people."

The young woman and the snake stayed together and talked all afternoon. In the evening, in the last light of the sun, the snake went back to the place in the river where the woman had found him when she was a girl, then he swam through the breakers and into the ocean.

The young woman watched his colors disappear, and she was sad, as if she'd lost a good friend.

STORY TREE AT KILCHIS POINT

I HAVE HEARD THE LEGEND ABOUT THE GREAT grandmother tree that takes care of native stories, holding them carefully inside her trunk for a long, long time. This is not only a legend about the oldest Keeper of Stories in the Tillamook country, it is also about storytelling. Being a tale-teller myself, I am determined to find the tree.

The Old Ones call the Tree People the One Leggeds. Though deep-rooted, they've been known to travel a bit. And they all look different. There are forest trees, family trees, history trees, legendary trees, ceremonial trees ... There are young trunks with their stories still attached, old trunks who have dropped their stories to the ground, whole groves of trees whose stories have been scattered to the winds by wild winter storms or burned to ash by fires or cut down to build houses, villages, ships.

I walk along the abandoned railroad tracks and into the woods. If I were the Story Tree, I would find a protected place, an ancient nook in the depths of the forest, and I'd call that home. For a long, long time.

After crossing a short trestle, I turn onto an old trail and follow it into the forest. Though it's a sunny autumn afternoon, these woods are dark with deep shadows. A breeze rolls in from the bay and makes the shadows sway. I squint and watch the One Leggeds dance!

I keep walking. Years ago, I met an old woman whose ancestors lived near here where the Kilchis River flows into Tillamook Bay. She told me about the tree as a way of explaining the art of native storytelling: "If the stories are well told," she said, "listeners feel invited to step into the narrative. They journey across the ocean and back again, up and down rivers and creeks, along beaches at sunset, through shadowy forests. They meet South Wind face to face. They watch Wild Woman dance in her winter lodge and Ice Man slide slowly along the coast. They hear the creak of Spanish ships as they sail into the bay. They revel in the adventure of each tale and dodge the dangers. In the end—if the story-teller knows his art—they come home to find themselves sitting in the cozy firelight under the sheltering boughs of the Story Tree. Though this setting is familiar as the place where the first story began, the night feels somehow different, and so do the people. When the last word is spoken, the stories are stored inside the tree where they safely await a new teller and a new telling. And there's always room for one more story."

In the dim light I sense movement, probably a critter who sees me before I see him and decides to disappear into the trees. Once I stumble across a pile of rocks, an ancient cairn someone built so many years ago it is now covered with moss. Once I slip-slide across a deep pool on a slippery log.

I follow the path and eventually walk into a meadow by the river. This must be the site of Kilharnar, the largest Tillamook village on this part of the coast. It's the perfect place to live: the river, the forest, a meadow full of sweet-tasting roots, the sea nearby with her abundance of food, a mostly-mild climate …

I walk along the river and down to the beach on the edge of the bay, then north, wading across the mouths of creeks. I gaze at the last bit of sunlight across the bay as it lights Memaloose Point. It'll be fully dark soon. Just then I see her, rising above the other trees, a giant grand-mother spruce that looks like she's been here since time began. Maybe she is the Story Tree. I turn back into the woods and the shadows and scrape my way through the thick brush toward the tree.

Like the Old Ones say, the One Leggeds are tricksy in their travels. I cannot find the tree I thought I saw. I swear she slipped away when I blinked, and in her place is a different tree. Nearby is an old fire ring and a bit of modern trash that has nothing mythic about it. However, I spot the beginning of an old trail that winds even deeper into the woods. This trace is a bit overgrown, but there is just enough light to find my way.

I follow the path past several giant trees, and not one of them feels like her. Evening is here. Shadows are fringed with purple twilight. Near the edge of the forest I pause under another spruce to catch my breath. I sit and watch the last colors in the sky fade and the first stars blink on.

This tree is not huge but she's interesting. Several large roots show above ground, twisting into mysterious shapes. At the base of the trunk is a hollow space big enough for some critter to make a lair in, or at least a dry place to crawl into on a wild, wet night. Yes, she's an interesting tree.

Now things start to happen.

I hear the creak of an ancient door opening slowly. I can't tell where it's coming from. I stand up and walk toward the sound. Shadows are thicker, and I put my hands in front of me to keep from running into branches. Instead, I bump into what feels like a wall. The creaking sound shifts. Now it's behind me. I walk back past the tree, and there's another wall. It feels like I'm inside a room. I walk around the back side of the tree. The creaking grows louder. I stare at the tree until my eyes adjust and make out a crack in the trunk. As the crack widens, light flares from inside. A figure steps out, and I recognize my old friend Coyote.

"What are you doing here?" I ask.

"Hiding," says Coyote. "Like my door?"

"That was a door? Looked more like a crack in the wood."

"Of course that's what you saw. You're not me!"

"Thank goodness for that. Who are you hiding from?"

"The locals. No one knows who I am. These folks think I'm nothing more than a bothersome domestic dog. They have no myths about the real me. I've been un-famed, turned invisible, a mythic hero shrunk down, a common … beastie. They've replaced me with some breathy guy who knows a few parlor tricks. South Wind is the villain's name."

"It's getting dark. I should go."

"How about a fire and some stories? It's lonely around here."

"We can't build a fire. Too many branches overhead. And it's been a dry summer. Too dangerous, and …"

Before I finish, the darkness is complete. But not for long. A few feet away, near the hollow trunk of the tree, a faint light flickers into a small fire. The flames grow and reveal that we are indeed inside what appears to be an Old Time native lodge. The fire and tree are in the center, and there is a hole in the roof large enough for both the tree and smoke from the fire to escape into the night sky. Perched on twisted roots are four figures who look like they just stepped out of a myth.

"Cool," says Coyote. "It's nice to have company."

I'm surprised that Coyote's voice doesn't startle the figures. They pay no attention to the pooch. For them, he's not even there. Instead, their eyes focus on me.

One is clearly a woman, and old. The wrinkles in her face are deep, her eyes even deeper, with a wild look about them. She glances nervously from one figure to another. With each glance, her face changes, exactly expressing the mood of who she's looking at. She expects someone else to talk. Anyone but her.

Sitting next to Wild Woman is an ice sculpture in the shape of a man. I see him breathing, slowly but deeply. He's so transparent I see firelight through him. He's worn smooth in places, and water drips from his edges. He looks like he's been around for a long time.

As Ice Man scoots slowly back from the fire, I notice someone else. He's a fidgety fellow. He stands up, walks around, and sits down in another place. His hands form gesture after gesture. Then he stands again and walks swiftly around the fire. He's always moving. Even his clothes are wispy, made of thin cloth that swirls and twirls with every movement. I can't see his face. His garment has a hood, and it's pulled down onto his forehead, hiding his eyes and casting shadows onto his cheeks. He whispers to himself. His words fly away before I can make them out, except for these two: "South Wind, South Wind,

South Wind," repeated over and over.

The only fellow that looks like he comes from some version of this world is a young man sitting close to the fire. He is draped in a robe. After staring into the flames, he pulls out a notebook and scribbles into it. When he looks my way, I see an Asian face.

He's the first one to speak. He stands by the fire, squints at his notebook, and says, "I gaze at the old woman's face. She looks abandoned. The moon is her only friend."

Wild Woman perks up and does a rowdy circle dance around the fire. The South Wind man with wispy clothes joins her, dancing two steps to each of hers. Ice Man glares and doesn't move a muscle.

Coyote says, "This is as weird as anything that I could dream up."

"Strange," I say, and everyone looks my way.

The man in the robe clears his throat and draws their attention. "I have more," he says. He raises his notebook and reads from the cover, "Poems by Bashō. That's me." He opens the notebook.

"Bones beaten white by harsh weather. I'll leave you to the cold winds that pierce your heart."

Everyone sits in silence.

"I'll tell you about the Lightning Door, and more," says Bashō. "I heard about it from a man who journeyed across the ocean to my home."

Everyone's eyes are on him. No one says anything. He interprets their silence as permission to proceed, and he starts his tale.

"I live on the other side of the sea. I was just a boy when a man who lived here along this coast came to visit my home. Here's what he told me about his journey …"

"We call it the Lightning Door," he said. "At the river's mouth the door thunders open. Flashes of light reveal the path across the sea. Then the door smashes closed so quickly that many a man who tried to jump through was cut in half.

"I wasn't the first one to journey beyond the sunset. Over the centuries, many made the trip. Each time they came back home to our coast, they described the ancient people who lived in bamboo forests that seemed so strange to us.

"One day, I decided to make the journey. I heard that Thunderbird lived close by and helped people get through the Lightning Door. Thunderbird was a huge condor, and when he flapped his wings, he made thunder. He lifted the door and held it open as I slipped through. Lightning flashed and faded, and as the sun shone again, I saw what I thought was a whale floating in the breakers. When I looked closely, I saw it was a giant canoe stretched with whale skin. As I got inside, Thunderbird perched on the edge of the boat, stretched his wings into a sail, and I started west across the ocean. That's how my journey began."

While Bashō tells the man's story, Wild Woman dances his words, her body creating each character, her face completely remaking its look. It's as if she swiftly changes costumes, switches masks. First the Lightning Door, stamping around the fire, her mouth opening and closing, then the far look in her eyes as she becomes one of the people who live across the sea, then huge Thunderbird, her arms wide, fierce eyes flashing lightning.

South Wind flies out of the smoke hole and whispers the story's antics from outside. It's hard to hear. But Coyote understands his lingo and he translates for me. "Now I blow and blow. Thunderbird turns his wings, and the canoe heads west. I blast north to make another story about myself."

Ice Man adds sounds to Bashō's tale. They seem old, from a time when the local language was young and words were scarce. Ice Man has a long memory, and making modern speech is difficult. Sounds come easy but slowly. It takes him a while to slip in a few words: "Time old winter. House it was. Ice before. Water after. People across. Back. And again. Time old."

I feel myself sinking into the story, drawn deeper into that place where myths and dreams talk to each other. I must have dozed for a moment. I hear Bashō say, "That's how he made the journey, and now I've traveled the other way, from my home to here, and here I share the story."

Bashō's story is finished before I realize it, and everyone starts clapping.

"Did I miss part of the story?" I ask Coyote.

"Maybe you'll hear it again sometime," smirks Coyote. "Or maybe you can check out the book from the Story Tree and read it yourself."

Applause fades into a deep silence. Everyone looks at me, like it's my turn to share.

"There they go again," says Coyote. "Ignoring me. Maybe you could tell them a Coyote story, and then they'd be able to see me. Something new that restores my heroic stature? How about a story set right here in these woods?"

I nod to Coyote and improvise …

A long time ago on a winter day, Coyote was wandering around Kilchis Point. The wind was cold. The rain was fierce. Coyote crawled up inside a hollow spruce tree, curled into a cozy ball, and fell asleep.

It would have been a long nap for most folks, but it was short in Coyote's mind. Centuries flashed by. Critters came and went. The Tillamooks arrived and built a village of wood houses by the river. John Doty sailed along the coast with Drake on the Golden Hind. Joe Champion became a neighbor in a tree of his own. William Doughty helped sign the Oregon Territory into existence. Dotys and Doughtys and Doughertys came to town. Some folks cut down a few trees and built a ship. Other folks cut trees and built an industry.

"Wait a minute," says Coyote. "I thought this story was about me. Get to the point!"

"Right," I say, and continue …

So Mister Coyote snored through the commotion, year after year. On one wild winter day, the grandfather storm of all storms descended onto the coast. The wind was jagged with ice. Snow blew in, piled up, filling the woods and blocking the trails.

Though the storm howled and raged and hammered his tree, Coyote slept on until his stomach gurgled and growled, and he woke up feeling hungry. He slid down to the hollow at the bottom of his tree. Where there was once an opening, there was now a wall of ice. He scampered back up, looking for holes, any way out. Nothing. He was trapped inside!

He talked to the tree. "Now listen here, Mister One Legged. I'm the boss of this forest, and I command you to open up and let me out."

The tree didn't do anything.

"Open up! Open!" Coyote kicked the tree a few times and yelled all kinds of things I won't repeat here.

The tree ignored Coyote.

He pounded on the inside of the trunk and called for help. "Hey, any fool passing by. This is Coyote. I'm trapped inside this tree. Come and get me out!"

Coyote put his ear to the trunk. At first he heard nothing, but soon there was the faintest flutter of wings as someone landed on a branch.

"Who's out there?" asked Coyote.

"It's me, Flicker. Got a problem, do you?"

"The storm trapped me inside this tree. I've got important things to do in the world. Drill a hole so I can get out!"

Amused, Flicker started drumming on the trunk. The noise was deafening! Coyote covered his ears. Flicker kept on. Coyote danced around inside the tree. Finally, he screamed, "Stop, you feathered varmint! You're too loud!"

Flicker glided away in a huff.

There was a small hole in the trunk, and Coyote stuck his eye up to it. Off in the snow, he could see Pileated Woodpecker flying from tree to tree.

"Hey, Woodpecker Man," Coyote called. "Come and help me get out of this tree. I'm Coyote. I'm important. There will be a reward!"

Pileated Woodpecker flew to the tree and inspected the hole. He tapped around the edge, testing the wood. Then he went full bore, banging away and making the hole bigger.

Coyote screamed from inside the tree. "Stop! Stop! It's too loud. You're hurting me!"

Pileated Woodpecker flew off.

Coyote put both eyes up to the hole and looked out.

He saw Sapsucker on a nearby tree, and decided to take a different approach.

"Mister Sapsucker, how fine you are looking this morning with your feathers flashing red in the morning sun."

Now Sapsucker was a sap for that kind of talk, and he flew over to Coyote's tree. "You think so?"

"Certainly," said Coyote. "And there's no describing the strength and beauty of your beak. It looks strong!"

"Like a hammer and a drill put together," said Sapsucker. "Want to see?"

"Sure," said Coyote. "Try it out on this hole."

Sapsucker went to work, hammering at the hole. Coyote once again muffled his ears and repeated his "I'm going crazy" dance. He yelled out the hole. "Stop! Stop! Stop! You're driving me nuts!"

Sapsucker flew off and landed on a distant tree and started smoothing his ruffled feathers.

When Coyote's head stopped ringing, he inspected the hole. "It's bigger," he thought. "Not big enough to slip through, but if I take myself apart and put my parts through the hole, I can put myself back together outside."

That's just what he did. First his feet, then his legs, then his tail, then his main body in parts, piece by piece, organ by organ. He was just tossing his intestines when Raven came gliding by.

"Haaaaa!" screamed Raven. "Look at all of this good stuff. I love intestines!"

All that was left of Coyote inside the tree was his head and his paws. He yelled through the hole.

"Now Raven, I'm going to need that stuff. You leave it alone!"

"Oh, it's Coyote," said Raven. "And here I thought you were a smart pooch. But look at all of this good stuff you're throwing away!"

Raven slurped and swallowed Coyote's intestines and flew off into the woods, chuckling as he went.

Coyote popped his head out through the hole, called for his paws, and started putting himself back together. The day was warming up. The snow was starting to melt. Even the ice around Coyote's tree was looking thin. Coyote went walking through the woods sniffing for something to eat.

He smelled smoke. "Hmmm. Where there's smoke there's fire, and where there's fire there's food." Coyote followed his nose.

He came to a field that people had recently burned. Sure enough, scattered throughout the burned area were roasted grasshoppers. Coyote's favorite!

Careful not to scorch his paws, Coyote tiptoed through the burned area scarfing down grasshoppers. But he couldn't fill up. With no intestines, everything he ate went right through him. He was hungrier than ever!

Raven soared over the burn. "Hey, look at Coyote. He's spilling out all over the place. We thought you were a brainy Coyote, an astute Coyote, a Coyote oozing with wisdom. Guess we were wrong!"

Coyote chased his tail and looked behind him. "Oh, oh." He came to a smoldering log with a bit of pitch on it. He took some pitch, rolled it into a ball, and plugged up the problem. Then he went on gobbling grasshoppers.

Coyote came to a place where sparks were still flying around, and his plug of pitch caught fire. Coyote scampered onto the nearest patch of snow where he could soothe his burning bum.

He heard Raven laughing in the woods, "Haaaaa! Haaaaa! Haaaaa!"

Later that day, people from the village came to have a look at the field. They were amazed at what they found. Every place where Coyote had leaked out, the first bushes started growing. These were wiry evergreens with sticky globs and fragrant roots. In honor of our furry friend, folks called them Coyote Bushes. And the name stuck.

Now that's the end of this tale.

◇◇◇◇◇

Coyote says, "That's a fine story. It shows me taking charge of the lesser critters who live in this place. In the end, I always win! And my name is everywhere!"

A bit of chatter breaks out inside South Wind's head, and he speaks it aloud. Here's how it goes:

"What's he mean by lesser?"

"I don't know. Coyote kind of ignores the bad parts about himself, doesn't he?"

"And what's this about Coyote Bushes? I heard a version of that story down south. It was tobacco plants he made!"

"Coyote Bushes are good. They're shifty like Coyote. They take on different shapes in different places. And aren't they also called Dwarf Coyote Bushes? That's even better!"

"Here's another thing. I've never seen a tree around here with a door in it."

"Open your eyes. It's this tree. If you stayed in one place for more than half a second, you'd know that the door is invisible to anyone but the one who lives here. At the moment, that's Coyote."

"You just made that up."

"Didn't! I heard the door slam when Coyote came out. That proves it's both mythic and real."

"Well, the story aside, this might be a good time to humor Coyote since he's taken up digs in our neighborhood. We might pretend that the story makes him look good."

"Right. Let's keep him happy."

Coyote doesn't hear any of South Wind's talk. He is wandering around in his thoughts. Suddenly he stands up, makes a series of gestures that suggest closing a book and putting it in his pocket. Then he scampers back inside his tree. I hear him rehearsing his story to a made-up audience. Smug with satisfaction, he howls, "A long time ago, there was an awesome hero named Coyote who lived inside a magnificent spruce with a magic door. He was the Big Boss of the Woods …"

As the fire dies down, the walls of the house give way to the forest. When I look back at the Story Tree, everyone is gone. There are scrapes in the dirt—not quite footprints—that lead into the woods and disappear.

Sunlight streaks over the hills and fills the forest. I walk along the edge of the woods to the bay. I find a good sitting rock, pull out a notebook, and write out the beginnings of a new story. It's my story this time … the story of where I've been and where I'm going and who I've met along the way. Coyote plays a minor role.

I write all day under the autumn sun. I pace up and down the beach, trying out words and phrases. The tide pushes and pulls. I watch the sun move over the ancient gathering of Tree People who cover much of the country around Kilchis Point. I picture the cairn in the woods, the village in the meadow. I gaze across the bay and beyond to a distant land across the sea. With the first streak of purple from the sunset, I walk back to the Story Tree. I'm ready to share a different story under her boughs. I sit and wait for the shadows.

THE SUN ROLLS
NORTH AND SOUTH

ONE OF THE NATIVE NAMES FOR THE winter solstice moon translates as Split Both Ways. While the days will lengthen, there are still lots of long, cold nights ahead. A mixed bag to be sure. It's a great time to be indoors telling stories. Above Deer Creek in southern Oregon, the sun rises over Mount McLoughlin, lined up on the solstice with ancient cairns built of columnar basalt. That night, between stories, natives gaze at the winter solstice moon with mixed emotions.

On the night of the winter solstice, the people tell this story.

One morning the sun didn't rise in the east. Far away in the north the people saw her break the sky into colors. She rose free of the mountains and started rolling along south, following the coast, splashing the waves with daylight. For a long time she rolled and rolled, and it was always daytime. Then there was another breaking of colors and the sun went down, far in the south.

When it was time to be morning, daylight never came. The people looked to the east, but there was no light. They cut firewood by torchlight and ate their stored food until it was gone. The ocean froze, and the darkness continued for ten days.

Then there was a glimmer of light in the east and the sun rose, sending colors across the mountains. The sun rolled across the sky until she got to her midday place, and then she stopped. For five days she stayed in the middle of the sky, then she started off again, traveling slowly toward the west where she disappeared in the waves. Next morning, she rose in the east and followed her old path to the west.

Days got longer. The ocean thawed. Fish that were good to eat swam onto the beaches and the people divided the food.

"Someone must be helping us," they were thinking. "Someone must be giving us this food."

My Circle

During my first year of storytelling, I wrote a poem about what I thought it would be like to spend my life as a native storyteller. For years, these words have served me well.

◇◇◇◇◇

when I was a boy
I sat in a classroom
my desk in a row of desks
under tubes of fluorescence

my Indian lessons were time lines
of wars and bad whiskey
the cavalry yahoo! of John Wayne
diseases fat as a textbook

now in these woods
my head isn't thick
with events

I am not an historical white man
I am not an historical Indian
I am not an historical anyone

I am native—

right now

I walk the curve of the forest
I listen to the breathing rocks
I listen to the swelling berries

and under the moon
the night croaking away
Coyote and I sit around
remembering myths

our native eyes watching
the wind in the darkness
pushing our circle of fire
beyond history

JOHN BEESON'S GHOST

IN THE 1850S, WHILE MUCH OF OREGON'S newly arrived white population was calling for the extermination of Native Americans, there were some who recognized native people as deeply spiritual. John Beeson was such a man.

In 1853, John Beeson arrived in the Rogue Valley by wagon train with his wife, Ann, and son, Welborn. Appalled by the treatment of native people, Beeson began writing articles and speaking in public about native rights. As a result, he was driven out of the Rogue Valley by death threats, leaving behind his family. He traveled to New York, where he continued to advocate for rights of Native Americans.

In 1857, Beeson published a book called *A Plea for the Indians*. This is a treasure of Oregon literature. In this work, Beeson used a style and depth of language that would not be heard again until the Civil Rights Movement a hundred years later.

During the Civil War he met with President Lincoln, convincing him to take on the plight of native people following the war. Unfortunately, Lincoln was assassinated before that could happen.

Eventually, Beeson returned to the Rogue Valley and lived out his life. He is buried next to his wife and son on a wooded hill near Talent, not far from his homestead.

For me, John Beeson's death is not the end of his story. Here is what

I remember about the night I visited Stearns Cemetery, where I met the ghost of John Beeson.

The dead are not silent. Some ghosts speak wisdom we ought to pay attention to. They pace the centuries, unsettled, searching for an audience willing to listen to their tales. Their stories are true on the deepest levels of truth, and for that reason, they survive. They are the teachings, the wisdoms, the humanity of what is known. They are the sounds of our memories and our dreams.

As a storyteller, I have learned to listen. I have discovered that each word, each breath of silence, each subtle gesture, every gaze into the soul of every story is sacred. I have learned to open my heart and my senses to what may be possible. In this spirit, I journey into wild places where stories draw breath. Drawn by some scrap of scribbling, a conversation with a friend, some strange and wonderful sound, a mound or knoll in the landscape, I pause in the place. I settle in. I listen carefully.

On an October evening, as a full moon spreads pale light over the Rogue Valley, I climb the slope at Stearns Cemetery, toward the hilltop grave of John Beeson.

I sit in the moon-struck shadows of three trees that circle the graves of the Beeson family: a madrone, an oak, a pine. In these trees, a restless breeze rattles leaves with a haunting whisper. The long-shadowed twilight invites a quality of unquiet that sends spirits scampering into the night. I hear words of stories swirl over each gravestone. I hear the unsettled voices of my own thoughts. Beyond the shadows, Coyote yips and barks on a wild run down the valley.

Here in this cemetery, in the company of ghosts, I wait for something unusual to happen.

No one remembers when Mother Landscape first appears. Perhaps it is just before the Rock People, the oldest ones we hear stories of. Whichever way we look, whatever words we choose to tell the myths, no matter how our memory-soaked minds try to make sense of where we come from, nothing seems tidy, as if creation is a mirror of our own lives made shiny by how we desire the world to be.

There are always a few things spread around to make the world out of: some curve of hillside, a scattering of trees, the cloud-reflecting river, a deep sky and stars beyond, and a menagerie of Animal People wandering up and down the rivers ... Coyote's Mythtime buddies.

Arrival. Hapkemnas the Children Maker shows up, and things start happening. The Dragonfly brothers journey up the Rogue River from the coast, fixing up the world and making it ready for the people. Centuries flow by. Arrival. The Takelmas settle along the river. Mother Landscape invites them in. They make a family. Centuries and centuries flow by. Arrival. Miners and pioneers. Mother Landscape groans a bit, but smiles and makes room. She adopts thousands into her family. A day blips by. Arrival. Loggers. Fruit growers. Mall builders. Mother Landscape tries to make the best world for all of her children. Her family is huge. She stretches her arms as far as she can around everyone. There seems to be room, but just barely.

Near the beginning of this sweep of narrative, Coyote shows up with his talented troupe of myth actors: Grizzly Bear Woman and Black Bear Woman, Medicine Fawn and Jackrabbit and Beaver, Panther and his brother Wildcat, the White Duck sisters, Mudcat Woman, Rock Old Woman, Acorn Woman, the Dragonfly brothers, and many, many others.

They build a house along the river and light a fire in the center of the house. They invite Mother Landscape and her children inside. Everyone dances to celebrate new friends. And later, in the dark of night, they gather close to the warmth of the flames.

From inside the memories of their experiences, from sparks of dreams layered with their most vivid imaginings, the stories begin, here in the house, spreading into the wide world.

"Wili yowo, there is a house along the river ..."

Mother Landscape adopts the stories, giving them a sense of place. With people and stories in her family, the place begins to make sense.

They call the river Gelam, and the word stretches to include the name of the people to come: Takelma, the people of the river.

As generations of people arrive and depart, for as long as any story-teller can remember, the stories from the family of Mother Landscape get told and retold.

Night after night, Coyote makes himself a star of legend and myth. He destroys ghosts that have been taking living people with them to the Land of the Dead. He dies and comes back to life. He gets stuck to Pitch. He gets unstuck. He takes himself apart to escape the tree that closed him in. He gets put back together. He runs upriver looking for women, downriver looking for more women, and as it goes, he ends up with fewer than he would like. Frog Woman is his greatest disappointment. Night after night this spindly-legged canine buffoon romps through the stories in pursuit of his various appetites, always a hero in his own eyes, always with just enough humanity to inspire us to search our souls.

But Coyote is not the only critter in the stories. Skunk becomes a disillusioned lover. Grizzly Bear Woman loses her children. Jackrabbit goes crazy, chops down trees, and starts the first war. The deer steal Panther's pancreas, but with the help of his brother, Wildcat, he gets it back, Later on, to the disappointment of Coyote, Panther marries the White Duck Women.

There are more stories. Mudcat Woman weaves a basket out of sun-rays. Rock Old Woman mixes medicine and keeps the culture healthy. Acorn Woman brings good food to the people. After their trek up the river, the Dragonfly brothers become the Table Rocks.

Night after night, huddled close to the fire, the people journey through the landscape of myth. And each morning, as the sun rises over the river and the stories pause for a day, the people emerge from the house and see Mother Landscape in a new light. They feel as if they have traveled far and come home again, not quite the same as when they left.

A bit later in the narrative of the world, on the 28th of September, in 1853, John Beeson arrives in the Rogue Valley with his wife and son after a long journey by wagon from Illinois to Oregon. He sees Mother Landscape, and he says:

"It is impossible to describe the joyful sensations of our company, on entering this valley... It was a picture varied with shadow and sunshine, lofty mountains and little hills, meadows, groves, and silvery streams, altogether more beautiful than a painter could portray, or even imagine."

After his relief at having come to the end of his journey, Beeson looks closely and notices the brow of Mother Landscape furrowed with worry. "We were soon apprised of the existence of war with the Indians and the death of several men. I earnestly sought to learn the cause, and found no lack of informants."

Though the story of Mother Landscape and her family becomes horrible beyond belief, a new voice joins Coyote's troupe of tellers. Beeson becomes the newest storyteller to seek the truth and share the story of this place he now calls home. On a September day in 1853, Mother Landscape notices one of her children, and she invites Beeson to come inside and share the fire.

In Stearns Cemetery, I sit near Beeson's grave. Twilight and moonlight mix and catch a few words on his gravestone: "Beeson ... a Pioneer." It is too dark to make out the other words.

Through the trees, I look out over the Rogue Valley. My memory fills in what I cannot see ... a hillside of oaks, the river, a sky full of stars ... I see lights blink on down the valley. I imagine them to be the sparks of that first fire reflected in the eyes of the storytellers. A breeze dances across this hilltop like a breath drawn in before a word is spoken. I listen carefully. Mother Landscape has arrived.

When the last light of twilight lingers, there is an opening, an opportunity to journey into the depths. This is the traditional time of myth telling. From twilight to the first flicker of morning sunlight, the spirit world reveals herself.

Telling after telling, we listeners sit by the fire, surrounded by depths of darkness. We open our hearts and listen carefully to each word spoken, to each silence between each word. A good story has layers of truth. It is the art of the teller to give life to each layer, and it is the art of the listener to open the door and allow the truths of each story to enter. Sometimes a story feels deeply unsettling, and we yearn for a new day. But often, a story that lives in darkness is the story we most need to hear, over and over, until the truth becomes clear and we find a way out.

White and almost transparent in the moonlight, with eyes that glow like light from dying stars, my longtime sauntering buddy Coyote steps out of the shadows.

"Thought you could sneak out of the house and make this journey on your own?"

"What are you doing here?"

"I'm always around. And I love a haunted graveyard with juicy stories."

"How do you know this place is haunted?"

"I know why you're here."

"Think so?"

"I know so. I'm as close to your heart as you are. And snooping and lurking are two things I do well."

"That's scary. You do more?"

"Scary? You wander among gravestones on a full-moon night and you think me showing up is scary? Yikes! I'll show you something scary …"

A cold wind rushes up the valley. Trees sway. Moonlight dances across the gravestones. I look back to Coyote. He has put on a mask. I recognize the face of John Beeson. Coyote steps into a splash of moonlight next to Beeson's grave and speaks with words drawn from Beeson himself.

"The following quotations may be taken as a specimen of the spirit in which Indians were generally treated. They are from an Oregon paper of November 10th, 1855: The Indians are ignorant, abject, and debased by nature, whose minds are as incapable of instruction as their bodies are of labor. They have nothing in common with Humanity but the form; and God has sent us to destroy them."

Coyote pauses, removes his mask, and speaks in his own words.

"This view is familiar among us critters—buffalo, bears, coyotes. Well, there's more, and it's scary."

Coyote puts on his Beeson mask.

"At first they find more excitement in shooting bears and buffaloes, than they did in the States in killing rabbits and deer. They grow ambitious, and begin to think it would be a great achievement to kill an Indian. The desire becomes strong to slay one of those whom their own savageness has converted to an enemy.

"On coming to a lake, an Indian man, with two women, was discovered catching fish. The Indian, with only a bow and arrow, nobly stood his ground until he fell, riddled through and through by bullets of his assailants. The terrified females were caught, and made to witness the cutting and slashing of the gory body of their murdered husband, by those who thus added brutal insult to their previous crime.

"On another occasion, a White Man being found dead, was supposed to have been killed by Indians. A company was made up forthwith, an Indian Ranch was surrounded, and all the inmates were put to death—about forty souls—including men, women, and children. The domineering spirit grew by what it fed on … excited to madness.

"An Indian girl in the act of fetching water for her employers, was shot, and her body thrown into the creek. An Indian boy, scarce in his teens, who was in the habit of visiting the shanty of some miners, with whom he was a great favorite, and always welcome, was taken and hung upon the limb of a tree. Two women and a man took refuge upon Table Rock. It was reported that they had killed themselves by jumping down its steep and craggy sides. They fell because they were shot, and could not avoid it. Their mangled, but yet living forms, as they lay on the loose rocks below, were so revolting a sight, that many began to declaim against such proceedings.

"Few listened, and this state of things continued until people got into a perfect frenzy, and they found sufficient authority to condemn to death all Indians in the Valley."

Coyote removes his mask. Still drawing his words from Beeson, he speaks slowly, as if he has seen a lot in his long lifetime.

"Let us listen to a voice from fallen victims, from bereaved families, and blackened ruins, and be warned! All these things are significant."

There is another rush of wind. As fallen leaves swirl into a whirlwind, Coyote slips into the shadows and is gone.

I walk slowly toward Beeson's grave and sit in the moonlight where Coyote had stood. I reach into my story bag and pull out Beeson's book. In the bright moonlight, I can easily read the words. I turn page after page, searching for some way out of Coyote's dark story.

Words left behind visit me over and over again. Some of the words are remembered and told as stories. Others are written down in books or dairies or letters. Sometimes the words are carved on gravestones.

I find these words: "Sacred to the memory of Isham Keith ... Born September 13 A.D. 1834. He fell in the battle fought with Rogue River Indians on Evans Creek August 17, 1853. This tomb is erected over his silent and vaulted chamber by his mother, who feels his death as the rose feels the blighted frost. Fearless he stood upon that bloody field, bravely, until his mournful doom was sealed. He faced the savage foe. The earthly hopes all wither at thy tomb. The fatal shot left naught for me, but gloom my son! that laid thee low."

These words from one who has suffered settle into my soul. I feel a mother's grief at the death of her eighteen-year-old son. These singular words rise from a feeling that is universally tragic. There is truth here. These words might have been spoken by a Takelma mother. Something close probably was. Perhaps her story was lost. Or perhaps I need to listen more carefully.

Sitting next to Beeson's grave, I turn the pages of his book. I no longer want out of Coyote's story. I want to go deeper in. At a time when the Rogue Valley was on the brink of insanity, John Beeson offered a path away from the madness. I turn the pages and find this:

"The Indian gets the elements of his faith fresh from the hand-writing of his Maker. It is presented to him in the ever-open book of Nature. It is renewed with every returning spring; and comes forth clear and bright in the light of every morning sun."

The moon travels over the ridge. Just before sunrise, it is darker and colder. I can no longer read the words on the page, and I close Beeson's book.

I sit and I wait for something to happen … and it does …

Beeson's ghost settles onto a stump. Shadows of madrones and oaks and pines branch overhead. The living room lights of homes are flickering flames down the valley. The air is still and the night is dark.

His voice begins like an early sunrise, faint light at first, then bright as a sunny day and full of the smell of trees.

"Some of them won't believe you," he says. "There are some who didn't believe me about the Indians in this valley because they didn't understand them. And there are some who won't believe you when you tell them we had this little talk. But that's no reason not to tell the story.

"They didn't believe me when I told them Indians were hunted like deer, about the lynchings in Jacksonville, that Indian women begging for food were shot on sight. They didn't believe such atrocities could occur in this lovely Rogue Valley.

"They didn't even believe me when I told them that love is the universal cure for the social wrongs that curse the world. Their disbelief followed me right to this grave.

"But the ones who did the killings knew. They threatened to kill me, my wife, my son. They would have blamed it on the Indians, and some folks would have believed them."

Beeson's ghost pauses. Sunlight grows in the east. I can read all the words on his gravestone: "John Beeson. Died 1889. A Pioneer and man of Peace."

When I glance back to the stump where his shape had been, there are only shadows. I call after him, "Was it you who said about the Indians that this nation was born in genocide and murder?!"

"No … no," he says. "That was Martin Luther King, Jr. a hundred years later. We dream the same dreams. We tell the same stories. Some folks didn't believe him, either.

"Now it's your turn to tell the story. And get some help, you'll need it.

And remember about love …"

The air smells like trees. The rising sun carries the ghosts of his words down the valley where they settle over the lights of homes where people are starting to wake up.

Many years ago, and here on this sunny morning in October, the words of John Beeson continue to offer a path away from the madness.

The dead are not silent. Some ghosts speak wisdom we ought to pay attention to. I am haunted by the stories of ghosts.

WORDS AT THE END OF A STORYTELLING

You people, you've heard enough stories. You'll need stories all of your lives, but too many at one time and your ears will grow long from listening to too many stories. And you'll have bad luck with rattlesnakes.

While you're alive, do something important. Learn the flowers. The way of the deer in the brush, the way of the birds in the trees and the sky. Learn the dances of the people and the music of the river. Dance the rhythms of the earth.

You people, find your stories and share them.

You people, keep the world going! Forever. And ever. That is all.